"Basil
tightly
with a nautical background... on par with the works of such recognized genre icons as Harry Whittington, Gil Brewer, or Bruno Fischer."—Paul Bishop,

"If you like such writers as Cain, Hemingway, Steinbeck, etc, make room on your bookshelf for Basil Heatter."
—*Miami Herald*

"Realistic, tremendously masculine, blunt in language and a thorough-going story."
—*San Diego Union*

"Naked and realistic."
—*Montgomery Advertiser*

"Written in a rat-a-tat tempo that never for one moment lets the story drag or the reader drowse."— *Bridgeport Post*

"Fast and ruthless. No punches are pulled."—*Worcester Telegram*

ANY MAN'S GIRL

by Basil Heatter

Black Gat Books • Eureka California

ANY MAN'S GIRL

Published by Black Gat Books
A division of Stark House Press
1315 H Street
Eureka, CA 95501, USA
griffinskye3@sbcglobal.net
www.starkhousepress.com

ANY MAN'S GIRL
Originally published in paperback by Gold Medal Books,
Greenwich, and copyright © 1961 by Basil Heatter.

All rights reserved under International and Pan-American
Copyright Conventions.

ISBN: 979-8-88601-059-6

Text design by Mark Shepard, shepgraphics.com
Cover design by Jeff Vorzimmer, ¡caliente!design, Austin, Texas

PUBLISHER'S NOTE:
This is a work of fiction. Names, characters, places and
incidents are either the products of the author's imagination or
used fictionally, and any resemblance to actual persons, living
or dead, events or locales, is entirely coincidental.
Without limiting the rights under copyright reserved above, no
part of this publication may be reproduced, stored, or
introduced into a retrieval system or transmitted in any form
or by any means (electronic, mechanical, photocopying,
recording or otherwise) without the prior written permission of
both the copyright owner and the above publisher of the book.

First Stark House Press/Black Gat Edition: September 2023

> Yet each man kills the thing he loves,
>   By each let this be heard,
> Some do it with a bitter look,
>   Some with a flattering word,
> The coward does it with a kiss,
>   The brave man with a sword!
> — Oscar Wilde,
>   "The Ballad of Reading Gaol"

FOREWORD

1

The county jail is ugly as an old dead whore. It smells of cabbage soup, of sweat, of misery. The iron walls are rusty; the cement floor is always damp. Sunlight has never been in the place; the hot air don't hardly move.

This jail ain't exactly escape proof. The way you get out is this: there is one shower in the place and once a week they take the prisoners in there to get the stink off. There is a big old iron lever like on a locomotive that unlocks all the doors. When they pull that lever you take a bottle cap from a coke or a Seven-Up bottle, or something like that, and when you pass by, you just stick that cap under the lever and later when the deppity pulls it down, it don't exactly close tight because of the cap. It clicks all right and it sounds tight, but it really ain't, and later you can give your cell door a nice little push, and if the hinges is oiled she will open like a bride on a weddin' night.

That's all there is to it. It's been done before and it

will be done again.

But you dassn't let on I told you.

The worst thing about this county jail is the smell of the old lady's cookin'. Cabbage soup. You wouldn't want to step in it. If they was any paint left on these old walls that soup would peel it.

Damned jailer and his wife live below. And a kid of three. Kid of three rollin' a ball and playin' around the cells. Now what kind of a way is that to raise a kid? For us old goats it don't matter no more, but for a kid it's different.

Like them four they brought in this mornin'. The oldest can't be no more'n thirteen. Tattoos all over his scrawny belly. And crap printed right across his miserable chest. Broke out of the county home and robbed a clothin' store. Set fire to the store just for the hell of it. Burned that damned old store to the ground. Now where will them kids wind up? Gonna wind up in the chair at Raiford and you know it.

What for they got me in here? They say I spoke improper to a white girl. She sixteen and me a old nigger of sixty or seventy, or eighty, for all I know. What would I want with her? What could I do with her? Lord knows I got no use for that anymore.

But I come off all right at that. Now if it had been Mississippi—there's a cold place for a poor old nigger—they'd of had me on a rope by this time and likely burned me to death. You can't hardly *think* about poontang in that state.

It's like this boy they brought in here yesterday and put next door to me. Nice lookin' boy, white boy, claim he killed his wife. Choked her. Well they's many a man chokes his wife, or would like to. But now they say he raped her first. How do you make sense of that? Who would want his own wife that bad?

2

"Did they book him, Sarge?"

"Why sure they booked the son of a bitch," the desk sergeant said.

"You think he done it?"

"You know goddam well he done it."

"Don't seem like he had no right to kill a beautiful piece like that. I swear I never seen such a body on a woman. I mean I've had me some ripe tail myself, but never nothin' like that. Boobies like pink melons. I mean they was a *crowd* down to the morgue to see her. Even dead they was more life in her than in my old woman alive. Even stiff I could of used a piece of that myself. Now why would a man want to kill a piece like that? If he didn't want her no more, why didn't he just naturally share the wealth?"

"I better tell Doc to lock up that morgue tonight or you just liable to be in there."

"Well now it's a thought all right. I mean—"

"Hell, boy, I know what you mean."

"I guess they'll fry the son of a bitch."

"They'll fry him all right."

"But the way I hear it, the evidence ain't no more'n what they call circumstantial. Ain't that right, Sarge?"

"Have I got to teach you the facts of life, boy? We got us an election comin' along here in about a couple or three weeks. State's attorney runnin'. Circuit judge runnin'. They all of them a little behind in convictions. Now this here is a nice neat case with no loose ends. That boy got no friends 'round here. Hell, he's a damn Yankee for that matter. That boy gonna die, is all."

CHAPTER ONE

Marty Waxman came in from the car carrying two big brown paper bags and said, "If you can tear yourself away from the newspaper long enough there are half a dozen more of these in the back of that station wagon."

Dan grinned up at her and said, "Now isn't that a hell of a greeting from a loving wife?"

"Sorry. I'm a little tired. The man who invented supermarkets should have been hoisted by his you-know-whats."

He held up the paper and said, "There's a case here for you."

"Every case is a case for me, except that nobody really wants a lady lawyer. What is it this time? Dog bite? Solid citizen exposing his genitals? Fishing without a license?"

"I'll fix a drink while I tell you about it. Gin and tonic?"

"Love it."

"You remember that kid Russ?"

"What kid Russ?" The long hot drive into Belle Glade and the damned wire carts and the standing in line for twenty minutes to get past the checker were taking their toll. It seemed like such a production just to buy a can of tomato juice. Why didn't a man try it sometimes, instead of sitting on his fanny reading the paper? No, that was hardly fair. He *had* been out in the sun all morning growing his bloody tomatoes. Looking at the sweat-soaked khaki shirt stretched tight across his broad shoulders she thought of how strange it was that they were really here in back country Florida and that Danny Waxman—man about New York's Greenwich Village, reader of Kafka and Joyce—should really have turned into an honest to God sweat-soaked cracker farmer.

"You remember Russ Perky," he said.

"I'm afraid the name still doesn't ring any bell. And what about those bags? Or do I have to get them myself?"

He turned and raised one eyebrow at her and said, "Here's your drink, sweetness. Cheers."

She knew he was annoyed by her insistence about the bags. This was, in some obscure way that she was too tired to fathom, an intrusion on his masculinity. Why were all men so damned sensitive that way? What made their infernal cojones the most important things in the world?

"I'm sorry, honey," she said.

"I'll get the bags and then I'll tell you about Russ Perky."

When the bags were lined up on the counter and she had torn them open and was stowing the canned goods on the shelves he said, "You remember that fishing camp out near Pelican Bay? We spent a weekend there before Christmas. I think it was our ninth or tenth honeymoon."

She remembered it now—a dusty back road out of Belle Glade toward Chosen and then up to the peninsula sticking like a finger into the vast belly of Lake Okeechobee and the cluster of Negro shacks, and then the fishing camp itself and its owner—a boy named Russ. "I remember it without any particular joy," she said. "It rained the whole time and there was a blonde in tight shorts who kept making eyes at you. Mrs. Perky, I think she was."

"That's the place," he answered smugly.

"If she'd pushed that chest of hers out any further she would have broken her back."

"I guess so."

"Well it's all over now. The poor little broad is dead. It seems he strangled her."

"Let me see that," she said taking the extended paper.

It was a front-page story. There was a picture of Perky looking ruffled and sullen between two towering state troopers. There was also a picture of the girl. Quite a picture. She was sitting on the bow of a skiff with her legs apart and the stem of the boat between her thighs. Except for very brief shorts she wore only a skimpy halter and as she leaned forward smiling at the camera, her full breasts three-quarters exposed. It was hardly the kind of picture calculated to keep the honest, bean-picking husbands of Okeechobee County home nights. And then, too, just to make it all juicier, there was the clear implication that she had been raped.

The story had been hastily written and there were few details. The substance of it seemed to be that Russ Perky—age twenty-four—fishing camp operator of Pelican Bay—was being held for the murder of his wife Lucinda. The dead woman had been assaulted and strangled and the body (nude) had been discovered by a Negro cleaning girl named Clara Williams. Clara Williams had immediately notified the police and on the basis of their investigation, Russ Perky had been taken into custody shortly thereafter and was now being held for the murder of his wife.

Good lord, she thought, all the ingredients for an absolute scorcher so far as the papers are concerned—rape, murder and a half-naked photo of a girl who would give Marilyn Monroe fits.

"I wasn't kidding when I said there might be a case for you there," Dan said.

"I don't know," she answered doubtfully. "The whole thing sounds sort of cut and dried."

"Oh come off it, honey. You know better than to judge any case by a newspaper story."

"What do you want of me, Dan? You know I don't practice anymore."

"That's just it. I want you to get back into it."

She shook her head. "No sale."

"Then why did you bother to qualify in Florida?"

"I guess I just thought it might come in handy some time."

"Well this is the time. Get into this thing. Get busy."

"He's probably got a lawyer already."

"I doubt it. He struck me as a simple sort of kid who wouldn't know which way to turn."

"Then the court will appoint someone."

"It's my guess that a court appointed lawyer is practically a guaranteed ticket to the chair."

"I don't agree with you. That doesn't necessarily follow at all."

"All right then, it doesn't follow. Look, I don't know whether he's guilty or not, and I won't hazard a guess. Frankly, I'm not even terribly interested in him. What I am interested in is you. I'm interested in your talents, your abilities, your mind. I am also interested in the shape of your legs and the delicate little curve of your …"

"Please, Mr. Waxman, I'll thank you to remember you are a married man."

"Look, kid, I'm damned serious about this."

"Why?"

"When you quit New York to come to this hell hole with me, we had an agreement. Do you remember?"

"No."

"You're being bloody difficult. You remember very well. The agreement was that we would give it a year to see if I could make something of my lunatic theories in regard to the growing of various vegetables. The year isn't up, but I'm not worried about it anymore. I think we'll do all right. What I am worried about though is you. You're a damned fine lawyer and I hate to see it all go to waste this way. You're making me feel guilty as hell and I've already got more than my share of guilt to start with. You don't have to add to it. Do this thing for me, Marty."

When Dan got nervous and intense this way it always made her uncomfortable. To steer him away from it she said, "What makes you think he didn't kill her?"

"He just didn't seem the type."

"As a lawyer I can tell you they hardly ever do. There really are no murderous types. Murder, and particularly the crime of passion, occupies a special niche in criminology. Did you know, for instance, that murderers, by and large, have a much higher intelligence rating than other criminals?"

"Then I should think just reading a newspaper account of this would light a fire under you."

"Why?"

"To begin with we know the people involved. But more important, it's a chance to work, to do the thing you were trained for. And not work on some damned piddling case of dog-napping or a busted fender, I mean the most important case of all—where a man's life is involved."

She was weakening, and she knew it. He could be so damned persuasive on matters unrelated to himself. "And if I were to go ahead with this as you suggest, what would happen to you and Meg while I was spending all my time on it?"

"Indispensable as you are, dear girl, we will not go hungry or dirty in your absence. Even a blithering idiot like myself knows how to throw together a steak and salad. I am also perfectly capable of seeing that Meg goes to the bathroom and brushes her teeth and gets into bed on time."

"Well it's not as if they will be trying the case in Hong Kong. I guess it will be right up there at the Okeechobee Court House."

"Sure."

"It will mean taking time away from your precious tomatoes."

"The nice thing about tomatoes is that they keep on growing, regardless. And that's especially true of hydroponic farming. You don't have to sit there and take the blasted vegetable's temperature every half hour. All it requires is a little judicious mixing of water and chemicals."

"Well, that's the first time I've heard *this* side of it," she answered tartly. "You've certainly made it sound complicated enough in the past."

"Could it be that you're really afraid to take a whack at this thing, Marty?"

A very good question, she decided. He could go to the head of the class for that one. As he had said, she had been well trained and had reason to consider herself a competent courtroom technician; but the brutal fact was that it had been over a year since she had touched a brief. She had been occupying herself with PTA meetings and television and last year's movies and the price of brisket of beef. She felt rusty and nervous, like a retired surgeon called on to operate again after a long period of retirement. Then, too, as a northerner and an outsider, she was afraid of what a southern judge and jury would do to her. The fact was she had lost all her confidence. She was scared. Dan was certainly right about that.

He was very sensitive to her moods and he immediately gave up the attack. He reached over to her and rubbed his cheek against hers and said, "Hell, kid, I don't want to be rough on you. I know damned well what you gave up when we came down here to take a fling at this idiotic business."

"You don't have to pin any medals on me, Dan. I'm your wife; I'm supposed to go where you go."

"Sure, sure. In theory that's the way it works, but in actual practice how many wives we know would be ready to make the switch as completely as you have done? I guess that's why I'm on your back about this thing—because I feel guilty about bringing you here. I don't want to see you stagnate and waste your talent and brains. I think you signed on for a bum rap with me, Marty."

"I wouldn't say that."

"Of course you wouldn't. But all the same, it's true. You needed me like a hole in the head. I'm nothing but a big ugly mug with a face like Yogi Berra's and I sweat too much and I've tied up whatever dough we had in this fly-by-night scheme. You should have married some nice kid of your own class with Brooks Brothers' suits and a couple of million bucks in tax-free securities. I can't figure what you ever saw in me anyway."

She felt a sense of weariness, of impatience. She was familiar with all his insecurities, and of late (was it the heat or the accumulated ennui of the years of marriage?) they had begun to pall her. Particularly this one—the one of self-deprecation. Because she was not Jewish and because she had always lived in the assured atmosphere of a reasonably well-to-do family, she was apt, at times, to regard his need for reassurance as a weakness, a sort of small boy yearning to be told that he could run faster and punch harder than anyone else. Perhaps, she told herself, if she had known antisemitism as a child, as Danny had, if she had grown up in a two-room apartment in a poor section of Brooklyn, it would be easier for her to understand this gap in his ego. But as it was it annoyed her, and it was at moments like this that she would have to remind herself of all his basic strength and stability.

There had never been any doubt in her own mind about why she had fallen in love with and married Danny Waxman. Of course there had been the big physical thing between them, but she was mature enough to know that might have existed with many other men. But right from the start there had been something else, something almost intangible. It had begun the first time she ever saw him at that party in Greenwich Village, when he had come in out of the snowy night, a big, hulking, young man with a long sad face and a shock of wild hair glistening with snow. And as he was introduced to her and shook hands with her, the sadness fell away and in its place she saw such a look of marvelous pleasure and joy that, perhaps, for the first time in her life she could feel herself to be of absolute importance to another human being.

That was the start of it, and later in the evening, in unspoken assent, without even asking her, he brought her coat and took her by the hand and led her out into the night. It was still snowing lightly, but the night was windless and not too cold, and the lights looked magical and diamond hard, and they had walked slowly along Eighth Street looking into the shop windows, and she had told him that she was working for her law degree, and he had stopped and taken her by the shoulders with his big gentle hands and said, "Somehow I never thought I'd marry a lady lawyer." Then he had bent down and kissed her—right there in the snow on the corner of Fifth Avenue at Eighth Street, with a bored looking bus driver watching them—and afterward they had gone into an all-night place for hot chocolate and talked as though they had never before been able to communicate with anyone, as though they would never find time enough to say all the things that were bursting to be said.

And next morning at breakfast she had said to her father, "A funny thing happened last night."

"Did it, Pumpkin?" her father said, not lifting his eyes from *The Times*. "What was that?"

"I think I got sort of engaged."

He lowered the paper and smiled at her and said, "*The New York Times* doesn't even mention it. What does 'sort of' mean?"

"Sort of means we have sort of taken a short-term loan on each other."

"Redeemable when?"

"When we get to know each other better."

"And how long have you known each other now?"

"We met last night."

"Oh."

"His name is Danny Waxman and he's big and gawky and poor but honest and he's coming here to dinner tonight to meet you."

"That's nice," he said returning his attention to the paper.

"Well I like that. Is that all you have to say?"

"What would you like me to say?"

"You might at least express disapproval."

"What would that accomplish?"

"At least it would show that you care."

"You really think I don't care, Marty?"

"No, of course not. I didn't mean it that way."

"I know you didn't."

"But don't you want to know more about him?"

"If you only met him last night, I doubt if there's much more you can tell me. Now why don't we let the whole thing go until tonight when young Mr. Waxman can talk for himself."

"But you will be kind to him, won't you?"

"I am always kind. It is virtually the only flaw in my otherwise brilliant courtroom method. I am too kind to the opposition."

"Poppycock."

"What did you say?"

"Have a nice day, darling."

"That's what I thought you said."

She had sweated wildly over that dinner, but it had come off very well. To her surprise Danny Waxman from Brooklyn and Jonathan Blake of the distinguished law firm of Mansfield and Blake had gotten along very well together. It was not true, as she had told herself fretfully, that they had nothing in common. They had at least one thing in common—Martine Blake and their shared love for her.

Next morning her father had said simply, "He's nice. I like him."

And that had been the real beginning.

In all the years of their marriage she had never known regret, never looked back. She had been proud and happy about him, but right now, tonight, she was too tired to try to communicate the whole thing to him again.

He had said, "I wonder what you ever saw in me anyway."

All she could answer was, "I thought if we had a child it might look like you."

"Well thank God it doesn't."

"Oh come here," she said. "Come here, lug, and give me a kiss. And for heaven's sake, shut up."

The school bus at the crossroads gave a thin far-off honk like that of a wild goose and Marty released him and said, "It would be very sporting of you to run up and get our child. My feet are killing me." Meg had just turned seven and bore a striking resemblance to a Botticelli angel. There was an eighth of a mile of lonely scrub between the bus stop and the house, and Marty was convinced that this was not a desirable place for young angels to walk alone.

"I always knew I should have married a younger woman," Dan said letting the screen door slam behind him.

While she was opening the can of tuna and getting the bottle of milk out of the ice box, Marty was thinking again about Russ Perky. Dan had pointed out that it could do her no harm to at least talk to Perky. In a way he was wrong about that. When she had left New York, she had put her career behind her. That had required a major decision, and to begin to practice law again now would mean a reappraisal of that decision, a questioning of all the things she had or had not given up for marriage. These were questions that it was not always wise to ask; for when you opened the door to that particular closet in your mind, all sorts of gremlins were apt to fly out. Yet with that knowledge she also had to face the realization that she had a tremendous urge to be active again, to fill her life with something more vital than the housekeeping routine.

All right, she decided as she heard them coming up the walk, I'll go over there tomorrow and talk to him. That much of an involvement I certainly ought to be able to cope with.

CHAPTER TWO

It was mid-morning before she set out to visit Perky at the county jail. The road wound around the west shore of the lake, and, although there were occasional glimpses of the great shallow bowl of water that was nearly forty miles across, she drove for the most part through unattractive scrub. The dreariness of the landscape was broken only now and then by clumps of unhappy looking cattle and rickety frame shacks. It was flat, hot and depressing. And the town itself, when she finally reached it, was not much better.

Although a few new storefronts had been tacked on here and there, the place looked pretty much as it might have looked around the turn of the century. The main street, divided by a broad ribbon of dead grass, seemed unnaturally wide for this day and time, and there was even the tumble-down remnant of the bandstand that one once saw in every small American town.

It was close to noon and not even a dog stirred in the heat-stricken town. She drove slowly around the deserted streets until she found the courthouse—a creepy, old, once-white pile constructed along the bastard Moorish lines that had been popular in the south around the turn of the century.

The office doors were closed, but there was nothing to keep her from wandering through the empty halls. The place was filthy and she had the uncomfortable feeling that it was probably crawling with vermin. The walls were smudged and the floors were dusty. Spider webs festooned the great arch of the rotunda and she had the impression that at any moment a flock of bats might whirl down into her face.

Yellow scraps of old lawsuits—faded reminders of anguish—still fluttered from the rotting bulletin boards. Everywhere there was a feeling of desolation, of mindless cruelty and despair. By standing on her toes she was able to peer through the grimy window into the courtroom, with its rows of ancient schoolroom seats and its American flag tacked crudely to the wall behind the judge's bench. It was like no courtroom she had even seen before, and she could hardly resist the impulse to people it in her mind's eye with a grim-faced cracker judge and prosecutor. The image of herself defending a client in such an atmosphere escaped her; she would as soon have taken a case to be heard on the moon.

Two hundred yards behind the courthouse—standing foursquare and brutally ugly in the sunlight—was the county jail. In front of it was strung a wash line heavy with unsavory looking underwear. It looked more like some squatter's shack than a jail, and smelled that way too. As she mounted the steps she was made nauseatingly aware of the rancid stink of cabbage soup.

Inside she was met by a tall, good-looking young man wearing a deputy's badge. He looked as though he had been carved in one piece from some hard brown wood. Behind him, visible through the open door to the kitchen, was an old woman with gray scraggly hair hanging loose around her neck as she bent over the stove.

The deputy asked if he could help her and she told him she was there to see Russ Perky.

"Why sure, ma'am," the boy said. "I guess we can arrange that."

Just then the gray-haired woman came whirling out of the kitchen snarling. "What's she want?"

"Wants to see that fella killed his wife."

"What for?"

"Claims she's a lawyer."

"I never heard of no lady lawyer."

"Well you've heard of one now," Marty said curtly.

"You got somethin' to prove it?"

Marty reached into her purse and took out a copy of her Florida Bar certificate.

"That don't mean nothin'. Anybody could have a piece of paper like that."

"Not anybody. Only a qualified attorney who has taken and passed the state exams."

"How do I know you're the one whose name is on there?"

She had had enough. "Now listen, you old bitch," she said icily, "in one minute I will leave this filthy rattrap that is a living disgrace to this county and go to the phone and put in a call to the state prosecutor's office to advise him that you are denying a prisoner access to legal counsel. And just in case you don't know what that means, I can tell you that it will raise even more of a stink than you have here already."

The deputy looked at Marty with open-mouthed, undisguised admiration.

"You don't have to get so all fired hot about it," the old woman said, turning tail and scuttling for her corner. "I just wanted to make sure, is all. You can't blame me for that."

As they climbed the winding iron stairway, the boy with the badge was chuckling to himself. "Ma'am," he said, "that lady is my granmaw and that's the first time anybody ever called her that to her face."

"I'm sorry."

"Nothin' to be sorry about. That's what she is all right—a old bitch."

Russ Perky was in the third cell. He was lying on the cot with his eyes closed. He looked much the same as she remembered him—the same slender young man with the open, boyish face. It was hard to imagine that so much tragedy, so many dark passions had entered his life within the past two days. Thinking he might be asleep and not wanting to disturb him, she hesitated, but he had already opened his eyes and was sitting up.

"I don't know if you remember me," Marty said. "My name is Martine Waxman."

"Sure," he said getting up and coming over to the bars. "I remember you. You were out at the camp with your husband and the little girl. Some time around Christmas, wasn't it?"

"Yes."

"That was when we had all that rain and the fishing was so lousy."

"That's right."

"How is the little girl?"

"She's fine. Look, Russ, I happen to be a lawyer and that's why I came here to talk to you."

"You mean about what happened at the camp?"

"Yes."

Apparently he had been holding himself under control because his face, which had worn a mask of wooden disinterest, was suddenly contorted and two large tears welled up in his eyes and trickled down his cheeks. He turned his face away from her and said in a whisper, "I don't want to talk about it."

"I'm afraid you'll have to talk about it, Russ. I'm here to help you if I can." She waited for some response, but he said nothing. "Don't you want my help, Russ?"

"How can you help?"

"I'm a lawyer."

"You are? I didn't know that." No more tears had followed the first two. He had regained his composure.

"Do you have someone representing you now? I mean do you have a lawyer?"

"No, ma'am," he answered politely.

"You haven't talked to anyone about your defense?"

He shook his head.

"Do you think that's wise?"

He looked straight at her and she noticed for the first time what a really astonishing blue his eyes were.

"Lucinda is dead, Mrs. Waxman. There's nothing anybody can do to bring her back."

"You still have your own life to consider."

"What do you mean?"

"Aren't you aware that they're holding you for your wife's murder?"

"That don't mean nothing."

"I'm afraid you're wrong there."

His knuckles grew white and tense on the bars. "Look, Mrs. Waxman, I didn't kill my wife. I just wish I could get my hands on the bastard who did. Anyway, I already told all that to the cops. As soon as they find out who really did it, they'll let me go. I won't need no lawyer."

"All the same, I think you should have counsel. Do you mind if we talk a little more?"

"If you want," he said, without any particular interest.

She asked the deputy to let her into the cell and when the young man had opened the door and then locked it behind her, she sat down on the filthy pad that was Russ's bed.

"Cigarette, Russ?"

"Thanks."

He seemed very polite, very sincere, utterly bewildered. Nothing about him fit her conception of a killer. But, she reminded herself, quietness and self-effacement in a murderer mean nothing. Some of the worst killers on record have been meek little umbrella-toting bank clerks.

"Even if I needed a lawyer, I got no money," Perky said.

"Let's not worry about that now."

"Are you a pretty good lawyer, Mrs. Waxman?"

"I think so."

"Did you ever handle this kind of a case before?"

"A murder trial? No."

"But you would know what to do?"

"Yes."

"Well, anyway, it's like I said. I won't need no lawyer. They'll let me out of here as soon as they find the guy."

"Did you kill your wife, Russ?" Marty asked suddenly, coldly.

If she had expected him to get angry, he disappointed her. Instead he looked at her sorrowfully and answered, "How could I kill somebody I loved as much as Lucinda?"

It's possible, she thought. It's perfectly possible to kill someone you love very much. But it's not very likely.

"Let me explain something to you, Russ. You're in a very serious position. You have been booked on a first-degree murder charge which means that the police and the state's attorney's office are convinced of your guilt. It also means that any further effort the police expend on this case will simply go toward substantiating the charge against you. They will not, as you seem to think, be spending their time looking for someone else."

"But how can they convict me if I didn't do it?"

"I don't know. It's too early to say. But in any case, you certainly need help. Even the courts recognize that. If you don't select a lawyer of your own, the court will appoint one for you. Perhaps you would be satisfied with that."

"I don't know," he said looking a little more serious and frightened.

"Do you want to tell me your side of the story?"

"If you think I should."

"I think you should."

"Where do you want me to start?"

"Start with the day of your wife's death."

"Well, it's like I already told the cops. There wasn't no guests at the camp that day, and I didn't feel much like working around the place, so I made up my mind to go fishing."

"What time was that?"

"I guess around eight o'clock."

"And what happened then?"

"I went up past Torrey's Island to the Slew. I caught a couple of fish there, but they was kind of small so I kept on up the lake to a hole I know that's almost on a line with South Bay. I fished around there for a couple of hours, but it was kind of slow. Along about noon, I finally caught a couple of fair-sized bass, around five pounds each, and I started back. Then I had some trouble with the kicker. I had to change the plugs and put a patch on the gas line. Anyway, it was around the middle of the afternoon when I got back to the camp."

"What do you mean by the middle of the afternoon?"

"Maybe three o'clock."

"And then what?"

"Even before I got to the camp, when I was still coming up the channel, I could see something was wrong. There was two police cars parked outside the house. I tied up the boat as quick as I could and ran up to the house. There was cops all over the place. That was when they told me about Lu. I said they must be crazy, so they took me into the bedroom and showed her to me. It was awful." He clenched his fists and she saw for the first time that his hands appeared to be unusually large, really out of proportion to the rest of his rather slender body. "Goddam that dirty murdering bastard anyway," he said contorting his face again. "Someday I'll find that rotten son of a bitch."

She waited for him to regain control of himself and then said, "Did anyone see you out on the lake?"

"Not that I know of. You know yourself, it's an awful big place. You could fish for a month around some of those back bays and not see anybody."

"Who called the police?"

"Clara."

"The maid?"

"Clara Williams. She's a colored girl lives about a mile up the road. She comes in sometimes to do day work for us. Lu was never much on housekeeping."

"What time did she get there?"

"About twelve I guess. That was when she was

supposed to come."

"What did the police say to you?"

"Just asked me a lot of questions."

"What questions?"

"Like did Lu and me fight a lot."

"Did you fight a lot?"

"I guess we did. I guess all married people fight. I know my ma and pa fought plenty of times."

"What did you and Lucinda fight about, Russ?"

"Oh lots of things."

"Anything in particular?"

"Sometimes."

"What was it?"

"Sometimes she used to say she wanted me to sell out the camp and go to Miami with her. Times like that, we had bad fights."

"Did anyone else hear you fighting?"

"I guess so. I guess Clara heard us."

"Did she tell that to the police?"

"I guess so."

"Anyone else."

"Pritchard."

"Who is Pritchard?"

"Runs the hardware store in Belle Glade. Used to come fishing a lot to the camp."

"How does he enter into it?"

"He was there one time when we had a real bad fight. I guess he already told them about that."

"How do you know?"

"I saw him at the police station yesterday before they brought me over here."

"I see. Well, I think you'd better tell me everything. Where you come from, how long you've been here, how long you and your wife were married, her background, everything. And you understand, of course, that if I am to help you, you must hold nothing back. Now do you want my help, Russ?"

"Sure, I guess so. Although, like I say, they're bound to find this guy, and when they do they'll let me go."

"I hope you're right. But in the meantime, it might be a lot safer to be prepared. Let's start at the beginning then. You're not from around here, are you? You have no southern accent."

"I come from up north."

"Where were you born?"

"Algonac."

"That's in Michigan, isn't it?"

"Yeah, but I didn't live there long. I was just a kid when my folks were killed in a car wreck, and after that I moved to Detroit and lived with my uncle. Detroit was where I met Lucinda. I was working as a machinist's apprentice at the Chevy plant then, and one night I went to have a drink in a place called the Blue Light Club...."

Once he began to talk, he was surprisingly articulate. The story rolled out in short, unemotional sentences. When he had first met Lucinda she had been working as a combination waitress and B-girl at the Blue Light, getting a percentage from the house on drinks she could cadge from customers. He had fallen instantly and wildly in love with her and less than a week after their first meeting he was asking her to marry him. Marriage was not, apparently, a very serious matter with Lucinda. Although she was only two years older than Russ she had already been married twice before. She told him, frankly enough, that he didn't have to marry her; she would live with him without marriage if he would support her.

But Russ wanted the full and official possession of her and he had insisted on the ceremony. The first year had gone well enough. It was in the second year—after they had moved to Florida—that the relationship began to go sour.

Russ had seen an ad in *Field & Stream* for the fishing camp at Pelican Bay. The price was high, but there was a big mortgage on the place, and he thought that with any luck at all he might be able to swing it. Lucinda admitted frankly that she knew little about fishing camps, and cared less, but the idea of wintering in Florida appealed to her, and so they had taken the plunge and wired a deposit on the Pelican Bay place, and then started south in their old jalopy.

Lucinda had expressed immediate disapproval of the fishing camp. It was too lonesome for her taste—she had thought it would be a lot closer to Miami—but still they had stuck it out. They had been there for a little more than a year at the time of Lucinda's death. He had been managing to meet the mortgage payments and even to put a little aside. If only Lucinda had been happier....

"Was that the only thing you quarreled about?" Marty asked.

"Other things too," he answered sullenly.

"What other things, Russ? It may be important."

"Men."

"What men?"

"You know how Lucinda looked. You saw her."

"Yes."

"Wasn't she the best-looking girl you ever saw?"

Marty nodded.

"No guy who ever came there could keep his eyes off her. Especially when she used to run around in those tight shorts. It got me sore. I wanted her to wear a dress like everybody else."

"But surely you knew that when you brought your

wife to a fishing camp there would be other men around the place."

"I guess I just didn't think too much about it."

"Was your wife involved with another man?"

"How do you mean?"

"Did she have a lover?"

"No."

"Are you sure? This is important."

"I'm sure."

"What do you think you might have done if you had found her with another man?"

The sullenness had gone from his face. He turned to her now with a confused, worried look and said, "Gee, I don't know. I guess I would have raised hell."

"Would you have raised enough hell to choke her to death?"

"Maybe I would. I don't know."

"Did the police ask you the same question?"

He nodded.

"And you gave them the same answer?"

"Did I do wrong?"

"I don't know yet, but I'm certainly beginning to understand why they're holding you. Russ, this may hurt you, but it's got to come out some time. Did you know your wife was raped before she was killed?"

"Yes."

"Did the police tell you?"

"No, but I know it all the same."

"How do you know?"

His face twisted and for the second time in the interview tears formed in his eyes. "Because I did it."

"*You* raped her?"

He nodded. "The poor kid. The poor darned kid. It was a hell of a thing to do to her."

"You admit raping her, but you deny killing her?"

His eyes were dry now and his voice was steady again. "I swear to you I didn't kill her. Here's what happened. Like I said we had been fighting a lot, and for a couple of weeks there, Lucinda wouldn't go to bed with me. I mean we slept in the same bed, but she wouldn't let me touch her. But at the same time, she'd go running around the house half-naked until I thought I was going nuts. It got so I was almost down on my knees begging her to let me make love to her. She said she wouldn't ever do it again until I sold out the camp and moved to Miami. I kept telling her if we sold the camp we'd lose every dollar we put into the place; but she said she didn't care, if I wouldn't take her to Miami there were plenty of others who would. That was when I hit her."

"This was early in the morning? Before you went out fishing?"

"Yes."

"How did you hit her? I mean with your fist or the palm of your hand?"

"With my open hand. Just a slap. Anyway, she tried to hit back—she had a hell of a temper—and I grabbed her to hold her and while we were wrestling around her bra got torn off, and when I saw her naked like that and all hot and sweaty, it was just too much and I grabbed her and got her down on the floor and made love to her."

"Did she resist?"

"I guess she did. She scratched hell out of me." He pulled up his sleeve and showed the raw red scratches on the side of his arm.

"Did she scream?"

"Maybe she did. I don't remember. It was all kind of confused."

"Are you sure you didn't put your hands on her

throat to keep her quiet?"

"I know I didn't."

"Then what?"

"After it was over I felt so lousy about it I couldn't think of anything except to get away from the place, so I took the boat and went out on the lake."

"And you're ready to swear in court that she was alive when you left?"

"I swear she was alive. She was in the bedroom crying. I could hear her through the door."

"And all this is exactly the same story you told the police?"

"Maybe I talked too much, huh?"

"Didn't they tell you anything you said could be used against you?"

"I don't know. I didn't think much about it. I was just telling the truth. That's why I told them everything. Should I have kept quiet about what happened with me and Lucinda? I mean about what I did to her?"

"I don't know. I guess it would have come out eventually anyway."

"Is it bad for me, Mrs. Waxman?"

"It's certainly not good, Russ. I'd be doing you a disservice if I weren't that honest with you. Barring any fresh evidence, you are the logical suspect. They have a nice neat package in you, and they'll do their best to wrap it up. But of course the trial may be something else again. There are many factors that enter into a trial—judge, jury, prosecutor and so forth. Anyway it's too early now to do any real worrying about it."

"You don't believe me, do you? You don't believe me when I tell you I didn't kill Lucinda."

She returned his steady gaze and said, "I don't know,

Russ. It seems to me if you were capable of raping her, then it's possible that you might have killed her. I don't say you meant to kill her, but you might have done it without even knowing it at the time."

"Mrs. Waxman, I could never have killed Lucinda. I raped her because I loved her too much. To kill somebody you've got to hate them. You got to believe me, Mrs. Waxman," he said with sudden desperate intensity.

She felt tired, buffeted. She said, "All right, Russ."

"Will you come back to see me again?"

"I want to think about everything you've told me first. But in any event, I'll certainly come back to see you again tomorrow. Is there anything you need?"

"I sure would like a shave and a clean shirt."

"I'll go out to the camp and get some things for you. Anything else?"

"I have a stamp collection out there at the place. It would help me pass the time here if I could work on it. It's in the second drawer of the dresser."

"I'll bring it to you. Do you want to keep these cigarettes?"

"Yeah, thanks. Listen, you won't forget to come back tomorrow, will you?"

"I won't forget."

"You promise?"

"I promise."

"Okay then."

"Do you want something to read?"

"No, I'll just lie here and kind of think about everything that happened."

The guard let her out. She descended the iron stairway through the same abominable miasma of cabbage soup. The old harridan in the kitchen pierced Marty with a shaft of withering hatred. Although the air outside was just as warm, at least it was moving, unconfined. She felt a strong sense of relief as she walked away from that foul place.

CHAPTER THREE

1

Dan poured gin into his Schweppes, made a face at her over the rim of the glass, and said, "So they think he's guilty. What do you think?"

"I can't be sure. He might be a very skillful liar, but I don't think he did it. He would have to be very clever and very daring to risk coming back after killing her and to admit the rape part. That would take a certain ingenuity that I don't think he's capable of. He's really a very simple boy. No, I'm inclined to believe him," Marty said.

"I'm glad, honey."

She held out her glass and said, "I could do with a freshener, please."

"I should think that could be arranged."

"How did things go here?"

"The plumbing burst, the icebox quit, the bitch had pups and Meg came down with the mumps."

"Dog, I'm serious."

"Believe it or not, we got along just fine without you."

"What did you give her for dinner?"

"Spaghetti and meatballs."

"God!"

"She loved it."

"No vegetable?" Marty asked.

"Lettuce and tomato."

"Did she have her bath?"

"Had her bath and went straight off to sleep without so much as a 'where's Mommy'."

"Do you still want me to go through with this thing, Dan? I mean do you really think you can hold down the fort here?"

"Of course I can. The only thing I draw the line at is the washing machine. I absolutely refuse to be checked out on that contraption. Now tell me about the cops. Were they nice to you?"

"Nice enough. Big, tough, unemotional. As far as they're concerned, he did it, and that's that. I asked them if they weren't going to look for another suspect, and they just grinned at me as if I'd asked an idiotic question, which in a way I guess I had."

"When is the trial?"

"It hasn't been announced yet, but by the look of the court calendar I'd say it will be between two and three weeks."

"That's a damn short time, isn't it? What's their hurry?"

"My guess is that it has something to do with the elections coming up next month. Both the circuit judge and state's attorney are up for another term, and I imagine they want to present a nice, neat slate to the electorate."

"Isn't that a pretty cynical approach for a broad like you?"

"I guess I'm really a pretty cynical broad."

"What you seem to be saying is that you don't think he has a chance."

"He has a chance, but not a very good one. And if he's convicted, it will very probably be on a first-degree charge. If that happens, he's had it. Here in Florida the death sentence is mandatory."

"Look kid, are you sure you want to get into this?"

She nodded.

"Why?"

"All the reasons you outlined for me this morning—plus the fact that he's really only a kid, and he needs help in the worst way."

"Good girl. Now what's your next step? Is there anything I can do to help?"

"Only what you've always done. Be there when the going gets rough."

"That goes without saying. And of course it works both ways."

"Thank you, sir. Anyway, I'm going up to Pelican Bay tomorrow to snoop around the camp. He wants me to bring him some clean clothes and his stamp album. Want to come with me?"

"I can't. Too much to do around here. The wash, the cleaning, the beds, baking, mending and ironing. I may even put up some preserves. How the hell do you put up preserves, Marty?"

"I feel rotten about leaving you this way, but after all, it was your idea."

"Of course it was. And I still want you to go through with it. Who knows, it may make a man out of you."

"What a hideous thought."

"Tell me, what was Perky's reaction to the idea of your representing him?"

"The poor little guy doesn't even think he needs a lawyer."

"I mean, did he talk at all, did he give you anything to go on?"

"As a matter of fact, he was surprisingly articulate about himself and his background. He was only ten when he was orphaned—mother and father both killed in a car crash. The thing with his folks knocked him for a loop, of course. Not so much his mother—he's quite blunt about the fact that he hated his mother—but he was crazy about his dad. From what he told me his father was a kind of gentle little fellow...."

With a lawyer's excellent retention, she was able to convey, almost in the same words Perky had used, the scenes from his childhood that had been unfolded for her. First there was the absurd name, Perky. The kids in school had soon enough taken to calling him Jerky Perky. At the time he could not understand why his father had not changed his name to Perkins or Smith or Jones. He had brought home a seemingly endless procession of scratched fists and bloody noses because of that damned name. Yet when he was older and could have changed the name himself, he had failed to do so. By that time he was stubborn about it and if it had been good enough for his old man, by God it would be good enough for him, too.

It was funny how as a kid he had never sensed that element of pride in his pop—probably because of his mother's contempt for the little man. When she was on the warpath, which was ninety percent of the time, Dad would flee to the cellar to escape her. He had a little workshop down there, and he would close the door and putter away half the night making things out of wood.

He had been a real artist with wood, Russ had said. No ear-splitting power tools, just the slow, steady motion of a plane or spoke shave, held in loving fingers and the golden shavings on the floor and the fine fresh smell of the wood.

"Henry!" Voice like a knife down the cellar stairs.

"Yes?"

"You send that boy up here right now. It's past his bedtime. I don't want him down in that damp old place anyway."

"We're just finishing up, just putting things away."

"I said now!"

"All right, Martha."

If there had been anger in him he had never shown it. Instead he had bitten down on it, transformed it into the marvelous things that came off his workbench. A lovely old captain's chair of softly gleaming pine. A little cypress bench with hand-wrought legs. A pair of book ends, graceful as gulls. All of them softly waxed and hand rubbed, never varnished. Each day he went off to the accountant's job he despised, and each night he returned to the cellar and the pool of light and his tools.

But *she* hated the things he made, much preferring the cheap shiny junk she could buy in Sears Roebuck. So that in the end all the pieces he had created had been given away to the neighbors or to people he knew at the office.

The night they died was black and rainy and he had taken the curve too fast in the old Ford and it was later shown that the rain had short-circuited the warning blinker at the tracks. All the same, it was not like him. He was a cautious driver, and he knew that curve and those tracks like the back of his hand. And even with the blinker inoperative, he still would have seen the red wall of the freight in the glare of the headlights.

Russ knew why his father had died. Because it was the only way he could silence forever the goading voice of that bitch.

There was a long moment of silence after Marty had finished the story of Russ's childhood and then Dan said, "It would be awful easy to practice a little home-grown psychoanalysis on a yarn like that."

"I think I know what you mean. Transference of the mother complex to the wife."

"Something like that. And there might even have been homosexual overtones, what with the love of the father and the hatred of women."

She shook her head. "Not from what he told me about his relationship with Lucinda. He could never get enough of her. No, he certainly had problems, but that wasn't one of them."

"All right, I'll stop giving you my half-assed theories. Just tell me one thing."

"Yes?"

"Now that you're a career woman again, who does the dishes?"

"When I'm here, I do. Is that the right answer?"

"Absolutely."

"While you bury yourself in the farm journal and cigar smoke, I suppose."

"Precisely, my love. And while you're at it, I could do with another drink."

"You know, I rather like you this way."

"What way?"

"Domineering."

"This is the eternal problem of the American female. First they want to emasculate the male and then as soon as they've got him where they want him, that is sans filberts, they feel nothing but contempt for him for being such a gutless wonder. The worst basic mistake any husband can make is not infidelity or wife beating or gambling away the family fortune—it's the first time he touches a dish cloth. From that moment on his marriage is cooked."

"All this just to get out of drying a few dishes, dear?" she asked mildly.

He kissed the back of her neck lightly and said, "I

adore you."

"Liar. Fiend."

"It's your bottom. You really have the most attractive bottom in the world."

"A little too broad, you said last week."

"That was last week. I'm older and more lascivious now."

"Hands off, sir. I have things to do."

"Well make it snappy, kiddo," he said, giving her a firm slap that sent a tingling sensation up her spine and made her feel less than ever like a counselor at law.

2

Eleven miles out of South Bay she swung west on 715 to Chosen and then north on 717 to Pelican Bay. The dusty back country road wound up and over the dike and then rolled down a little incline to Perky's camp. The small white house was half-obscured by Australian pines. As she stepped out of the car, the first thing she noticed was the intense quiet, broken only by the mournful sighing of the wind in the pine boughs. No wonder Lucinda had been restless here; it was a creepy, melancholy place tucked away at the back end of nowhere.

Hansen, the police caretaker, a small wiry man sliding not too gracefully into middle age, was fishing off the dock with a cane pole. When Marty told him what she was there for, he gave her a surly nod and said, "Help yourself."

She went through the kitchen into the bedroom and began to collect the stuff Russ had wanted. The shirts were under the socks and the stamp album was under the shirts. She dug it out and put it aside. In the next drawer down she found a .38 revolver and an unopened package of contraceptives in a foil wrap. Both objects made her uneasy. She was closing the drawer when she heard again the sighing of the wind in the pines and then the clank of the screen door and the whisper of steps in the kitchen. Her heart leaped into her throat.

She turned to face the man coming through the doorway and saw with relief that it was only Hansen. The wrinkled brown face that managed somehow to look like a lecherous prune grinned at her, and he asked in a dry voice, "Find what you want?"

She pointed at the shirts and the stamp album and said, "I'm taking these back to Mr. Perky."

His eyes flicked past the gun and the neat little foil package and he said, "They was somethin' else here might interest him more'n them stamps."

He opened the bottom drawer and took out a black leather photograph album and handed it to her.

Rummaging through the place, she thought. He has no business doing that. I'll have to speak to the sheriff about that, although it probably won't do any good.

She took the extended album from his hand and flicked it open. The pictures were all of Lucinda Perky. On the first few pages were the usual beach snapshots, but as she turned past them she felt a sudden sense of shock. There was a picture of Lucinda in the nude, a studio shot softly lit and carefully posed. Looking at it, she could not help but feel a sense of her own inadequacy. What a really astonishing figure the dead girl had possessed.

After that there were many other pictures, each more revealing. Lucinda dressed only in long black stockings. Lucinda stepping out of a pair of panties. Lucinda, cuddly as a kitten, curled naked on a couch with a phone in her hand and lips pursed invitingly. Lucinda draped engagingly along the banister of a staircase. Lucinda floating in a swimming pool with a filmy shirt plastered to erect nipples.

They were all studio prints, glossies, the kind that are mailed in plain envelopes. Bedroom eyes, wide, inviting mouth. Body falling naturally and with not the slightest inhibition into all the attitudes of sex. At one time or another, Marty reflected, she must have made quite a good living at this sort of thing. No wonder the fishing camp at Pelican Bay had seemed dull.

She was aware that Hansen was watching her face and she felt herself blushing. She closed the album and slipped it back into the drawer. The atmosphere of the room was suddenly charged with high voltage. She felt that if she remained there another minute he would try to put his hands on her. That was why he had slipped in to show her the album, to excite her, to see what her reaction would be. There was something about this house—the unmade bed—the recent memory of rape and murder ... She grabbed up the shirts and the stamp album and darted into the kitchen and through the doorway. All the way to the car she could feel Hansen's bright, wise, animal-like eyes boring into her back.

Oh man, lookit them crazy kids. They gonna bust right out of this ole jail. Done used that bottle cap trick. That gonna get them nowhere. They gonna be out a couple hours and maybe steal a gun somewheres and somebody gonna get shot up and maybe killed and then you know where them kids gonna be. Po damned white boys. Nothin' but babies, even if that one got that word tattooed cross his chest. Where they goin'? Goin' straight to hell, is where.

They got the door open now. I could go with them, but not me. Not this ole nigger. Too ole to go runnin' round this country with every crazy white man lookin' to put a bullet in me. Too ole a fox for that. I just sets me right here and lets them go.

Look lak that other white boy stayin' here too. One that done kill his wife. Now that is somethin' else. That boy got any sense he just better up and run. Else they burn him. That's fo sure.

4

Marty could sense the excitement as she drove up to the jail. Three state police cars, looking square and determined as bull dogs, were parked outside. She shut off the ignition and dropped the keys into her purse and walked to the steps. This time she was not stopped by the young deputy, nor by the old lady of the cabbages, but by a state trooper whose behind, tucked into tight pants, looked as broad and stately as that of a Percheron.

"What do you want here, miss?" the trooper asked.

She explained her mission and said, "What's going on, anyway?"

"Jail break."

"When did all this happen?"

"Some time last night. But don't worry, your boy is still here. He could have got away with the rest of them easy enough, and I guess maybe he would have been smarter if he had, but any way he stayed. The ones who got away were that bunch of kids from the Home. Your guy is still in his cell."

He let her by and she went up the winding iron stairway. Russ was sitting on his cot. He came to the bars when he saw her and she handed him the shirts and the album of stamps.

"I hear you had some excitement here last night," she said.

"A bunch of crazy kids broke out."

"Couldn't you have gone with them, Russ?"

"I guess I could have."

"Why didn't you?"

"I ain't done nothin'. Why should I run off?"

If she had entertained any lingering doubts about his innocence, this eliminated them. No man, no guilty man that is, facing a trial for his life would have the courage to stay behind and take his chances when he might so easily have escaped. Not unless he were a great deal cooler and cleverer than Russ Perky. No, if Russ had killed his wife, he would have run like the wind when he had the chance. Very likely this could be used to good effect on the jury. It could be brought out in her summation.

"When are they gonna try me, Mrs. Waxman?" he asked.

"I don't think it will be very long, Russ. Not more than two or three weeks. Unless I ask for a delay."

"I don't want a delay. I want to get it over with. I want to get out of this rattrap."

"Very likely they'll set a date for it today. I'll let you know."

"So you're my lawyer now, huh?"

"I guess I am. Unless you fire me."

"Oh I wouldn't do that."

"Is there anything more you need?"

He shook his head. "Now that I can play around with the stamps, I can keep busy."

"Don't you have some family or friends who ought to be notified?"

"Like I told you, there's no family. And I guess I never had much time for friends."

"What about Lucinda's family?"

"I don't know where they are. She never mentioned them. She ran off when she was just a kid. Anyway, the way things are I don't guess they'd care much for me."

"I'll be in and out to see you as often as possible. If you want to reach me for any reason in the meantime, this is my home phone. I imagine you can get someone here to put a call through for you."

"When is the—funeral?"

"Tomorrow."

"They burying her here someplace?"

"Yes."

"Will you be there?"

"Do you want me to, Russ?"

He nodded. "Maybe you could bring some flowers. Kind of like from me. So she won't be so alone."

"Of course."

Again the tears formed in his eyes and he turned away from her. Since there was little she could do to comfort him, she left him with his grief.

5

A fitting day for a funeral. Black umbrellas in the steamy rain. Some faces that she knew and others that were strange to her. A few had come to mourn, but the rest were there out of morbid curiosity. Ashes to ashes, dust to dust.... Farewell, Lucinda. Beautiful, unhappy Lucinda. Clump of earth on coffin.

A young, good-looking Negro. Tears on her dark

cheeks. That must be Clara Williams, the girl who had done house work for them. Beside her an enormously fat colored woman who stands bareheaded in the rain, disdaining the held umbrella.

A wiry man in a dark suit wearing steel-rimmed glasses fogged by moisture. He holds his thin lips pursed like a trap. She recognizes him as Pritchard, owner of the hardware store. Russ had mentioned that Pritchard had testified against him to the police. Very likely he will be called as a prosecution witness. She examines him curiously. His grief, if any, is not evident.

Beside Pritchard a stocky, fair-haired man who is a stranger to her. He holds himself firmly, but his face is not as rigid as Pritchard's. A shadow of something that seems less than sorrow but more than simple interest trembles his heavy jaw. She wonders who he is.

It is over now and they are beginning to turn away. She moves forward to lay Russ's flowers at the head of the open grave. The long narrow box seems meaningless; it is hard to imagine Lucinda dead in it, that magnificently vital body forever still.

The flowers are touched with reddish mud. The drizzle whispers on the packed earth. She goes down the path to her car. The stocky, fair-haired man is getting into a faded Chevrolet. He drives off without a backward glance.

Farewell, Lucinda.

CHAPTER FOUR

1

"I just want to ask you a few questions, Clara," Marty said.

The girl's big eyes jumped. "About what?"

"About the Perky case."

The colored woman stared down at her fingers as if she had never seen them before. "I don' know nothin' 'bout it."

"But you worked for them. And you told the police about their quarrels. Apparently you knew enough for that."

"Them police scare me. They ask me them questions and I just say, 'yas, suh'."

"You mean what you told them wasn't the truth?"

"I ain't tole no lies. Jus' tole what I saw and heard, is all. Don' know nothin' more 'bout it."

"Have you got something against Mr. Perky?"

The girl shook her head. She was tall and darkly handsome, statuesquely built. Apart from her present sullenness she was a very pretty girl. "I got nothin' against him. He always treat me all right."

"Then why don't you want to help him? There may be some little thing you can tell me that might be very useful."

Stubborn silence.

"Well at least you can tell me about their quarrels since you've already told that to the police. What did they quarrel about mostly?"

"Mistuh Russ got green eyes."

"You mean he was jealous?"

Clara nodded.

"Were any names mentioned?"

Clara gave a little jump as though she had been touched with a charged wire. Her eyes rolled. She said, "Tole them police all I know. Don' know nothin' more. Ain' no use for you to keep askin' me. You got to leave me alone. Anyway, I can't stand here talkin' to you. I got to go to my job now."

"You have a new job?"

"Yes'm."

"Where?"

"Mistuh Pritchard's hardware sto'."

"If you're a few minutes late, I'll explain to Mr. Pritchard."

"Don' do that!" Clara said violently. "Don' you mention it to him."

"All right," Marty said reassuringly. "I won't tell him I talked to you. But Clara, don't you know Mr. Russ didn't kill his wife? Do you want to see an innocent man convicted for something he didn't do? Don't you realize that by keeping quiet you may be hurting him very badly?"

"I don' want to hurt him. Don' want to hurt nobody."

"Then you must tell me what you know."

"Don' know nothin'. I done tole you that again and again and again. You got to leave me alone now. Mistuh Pritchard gonna be mighty sore if he find me talkin' to you."

"Why should Mr. Pritchard be angry?"

Tears in the great dark eyes. "Please. Please leave me alone."

"All right. I won't bother you anymore."

"When you sees Mistuh Russ, tell him I'm sorry."

"You'd better tell him yourself, Clara. That is, if you have the courage."

2

Lou Tayler came out to the row of gas pumps and spat the cigarette butt out of his mouth and said, "How many?"

"Fill her up, Lou," Dan said.

Tayler was a giant of a man with massive bronzed forearms and a huge frame. Dan had been buying gas from him for the better part of a year now and he usually got a smile and a, "Howdy, Mr. Waxman." Now Tayler bent sullenly over the tank without so much as a glance in his direction.

"How's the front?" Lou growled. Usually he raised the hood and checked the oil and water without asking.

"What's the matter, Lou?" Dan said. "Mrs. Tayler giving you a hard time?"

"She don't give me a hard time. No woman gives me a hard time. I don't have to take no crap from nobody."

"Okay. Okay. How are you fixed for cokes? Got a cold one?"

"In the machine."

"How about you? Care for one?"

Tayler shook his head negatively and stalked off.

Well I'm damned, Dan thought. Whatever it is, he's got it bad.

Dan got out of the car and walked over to the coke machine. He deposited ten cents and the machine growled, whupped and burped forth a bottle. As he was uncapping it and raising it to his throat he heard voices from inside the shack.

"Sheeny bastard," a man's voice said.

Dan slowly lowered the bottle and stood rigid. He felt himself going cold all over. He had not heard the term sheeny since his childhood on the streets of Flatbush. Sheeny, hebe and kike were the terms hurled at him then by the street gangs. Since he had grown to manhood he had never heard them again. Now it was as though the clock had been turned back. And despite himself, he felt again the old sensation of nameless terror. All his life he had hated violence, had crossed streets and ducked through back alleys to avoid it. For the most part he had been successful in escaping it. Now he would have to do the same thing again, put down the coke bottle, walk easily back to the car as though he had heard nothing and drive off with the bitter cud of humiliation sticking in his craw.

It was too much. Too damned much. Pointless, senseless, blind hatred. He knew from experience that if he walked away from this thing now, turned his back on it and tried to pretend it had never happened, he would hate himself, not only in the morning, but all night long as well.

Dan took his time finishing the coke and then put the bottle in the rack and walked, not to his car, but back into the shack. There were two men in there besides Tayler. He did not know their names, but he had seen them lounging around town at one time or another. Loafers. Lean, lantern-jawed men with small eyes and tight cracker mouths. They stared at him with open, undisguised hostility.

For a long moment no one said anything. Finally Dan blurted out, "Lou, what the hell is going on here?"

"Ain't nothin' goin' on. You come for gas and you got it. Man runs a service station, he's got to sell to anybody. Even niggers and Jews."

"I ought to bust your goddam head for talking to me that way."

The giant stood up and made a fist the size of a

cannon ball and said, "Why don't you try to bust my head, Mr. Waxman? I would purely love to see you try it."

The other two men had moved a few inches to either side of Dan so that he was suddenly uncomfortably aware that he was nearly surrounded. Knowing that he would not fight, would not risk a broken skull at the hands of these slack-jawed cretins, he quickly stepped backward so that only the open doorway was behind him.

"All right, Tayler," Dan said. "You and your lousy gas station can go to hell. But before I go I want you to answer one question for me. Why is it that for the past year you've been taking my money with a smile? Why did you suddenly turn on me today?"

"We got us a nice quiet town here," Tayler said. "Or did have anyway. Our niggers here know their place and know to keep in it. We don't need no New York Jews comin' down here to put no ideas in their heads."

"What the devil are you talking about, man? What ideas have I put in anybody's head?"

"Maybe not you but that woman of yours. She's been talkin' to that nigger gal works for Pritchard. Tryin' to get her to stir up a mess of trouble at that damned trial. We don't want that. Don't want no niggers messin' in white folk's business. That nigger gal know what's good for her she'll keep her damned mouth shut, else somebody will put a fist in it. And the same goes for you too."

"How much do I owe you, Tayler?"

Tayler looked at the pump and said, "You can read."

Blind with rage, his hands shaking, Dan took three dollars out of his pocket and threw the money down on the floor. Then he turned and walked to his car and got in and drove off.

His heart was pounding as though it would burst. He beat at the wheel with his fist. He cursed loud and long at the rushing wind.

It was no good telling himself that he had done the smart thing, that there was no use getting yourself killed when the odds were so obviously against you. The fact remained that he had run away from it again, gone scuttling off through the back alleys with his tail between his legs. The sense of shame and humiliation that he had known as a boy was ten times stronger now. There was only one thing he could do; he could make damned sure never to tell Marty about it. No one, not even Marty, could be expected to understand what this did to him—it was a slow poison in his veins that he would have to live with all by himself.

When Marty came that evening she was able to detect at once the heaviness, the somberness in him. His face had always been transparent, an undisguised register of his moods. It was one of the things she had first noticed about him, and that she had loved. To her, the idea of living with some stolid creature where the heart and mind were concealed by an emotional wall was horrible. Thus, from long practice, she was able to see at once that something had struck deep at him.

But at first he would not talk about it. He put her off by saying only that he was tired and had a headache. When she persisted in asking him what was wrong, he seemed to change the subject by saying, "I hear you've been talking to the Perky's former maid."

"How did you hear that?"

"Someone mentioned that they had seen you two together. Did you have any luck with her?"

"Not much, I'm afraid. She seemed terribly frightened."

"Of what?"

"Nothing specific. Maybe it was me. I never knew I was quite so formidable."

"You've got to remember that she's colored, and that that puts her in a damned delicate position."

"Aren't you over-dramatizing? We're not talking about the KKK, you know."

"We may be talking about something that's not such a long way from it. These are simple people, and when they become confused and alarmed over something, their response is apt to take a simple and primitive form."

"Are you suggesting that they may lynch me because I had the temerity to question someone whose testimony may be decisive?"

"Of course not. I was just trying to point out to you one of the things you're up against. Look, honey, I don't want to make a big thing out of this, so why don't we just forget it. Maybe you're right; maybe I'm exaggerating."

He had realized that if he kept on with it, she would be astute enough to understand that something had alarmed him. Such a realization would of course be a serious handicap to her during the trial. Anyway, he would have to invent some excuse to keep her away from Tayler's garage. He decided to tell her simply that he had learned that Tayler had been adding kerosene to his gas. It was probably a reasonable supposition anyway.

3

The secretary said, "The Judge will see you now," and Marty got up and went into the inner room where Circuit Judge Grady was waiting for her.

The room was old-fashioned, cool, shadowy. The walls were lined with dusty-looking law books, the leather chairs were cracked and darkened by time. The judge himself, a stage caricature of the southern politician, was almost too good to be true—a mountain of a man with a booming voice, florid face and neatly combed gray hair. He wore a white cotton suit, white silk socks and white shoes. The sheer physical mass of him and the power and energy burning out of his small blue eyes were impressive. As he sat back in his chair, his great belly lay in his lap like a melon. Before going to fat he must have been what was known in the old days as a fine figure of a man.

While they talked, the judge cleaned his fingernails with a pearl handled penknife, blew his nose in a white silk handkerchief, picked his teeth with an old-fashioned gold toothpick and wound and rewound his heavy gold pocket watch.

All in all, he was polite, hearty and reassuring. Several times he called her honey. Their discussion was, of course, of a very general nature, but she had the feeling that he was probably honest enough and at least familiar with the laws of circumstantial evidence.

When he escorted her to the door, he kept his hand on her arm and once let it slide down over the curve of her back. There was, she felt, a little more in this than just southern courtesy. He was probably not as old as she had thought. Obviously he still had an eye and a roving hand for the ladies. This might be a plus for her, and she made up her mind to take advantage of it. She would need all the help she could get in this trial, even down to a tight-fitting dress. If the Honorable Patrick was an impressionable man, she would do her best to make the right impression on him.

The trial was now less than twenty-four hours away, and that night, for the first time in weeks, she went to bed with a feeling of slightly renewed confidence.

4

The phone bell splintered the silence. Dan put down the book he'd started in hopes of diverting his worried thoughts from Marty and Russ and the trial. He reached for the instrument. The voice that answered his hello was soft, feminine, very southern.

"Mist' Waxman?"

"Yes?"

"Is Miz Waxman there?"

"I'm sorry, she isn't."

"She over to the courthouse?"

"Yes."

"They holdin' trial fo' Mist' Russ?"

"That's right. Who is this calling?"

Uncertainty crept like an almost visible mist over the wire.

"Who is this?" he repeated.

Marty had mentioned a colored girl named Clara Williams who had worked for the Perkys.

"Clara Williams?"

"Yes, suh."

He waited for her to go on, but when she said nothing he asked, "Can I take a message for Mrs. Waxman?"

"You tell her...." There was a pause and then she came back on with sudden urgency in her voice. "Can't talk good here. You tell her Aunt Bessie...."

He heard the sudden inhalation of her breath and then silence as the phone went dead.

5

Clara replaced the phone quickly when she heard Gus Pritchard's steps. She would know them anywhere. He was a small man but he strutted big, as if he owned the world. He walked like a proud rooster, stiff-legged, chest out. Even before he appeared in the doorway, she had the sinking feeling that she had not been quick enough.

"Everythin' quiet here, Clara?"

"Yes, suh."

"I thought I heard you talkin' to someone."

"No, suh."

"No phone calls?"

"No, suh."

"You sure about that, Clara?"

"I'm sure, Mistuh Gus."

"You remember our agreement, don't you?"

"Yes, suh."

"That you were not to do any talking to that New York Jew lady."

"I remembers."

"It's not that I have anythin' to hide, but I just don't want her comin' 'round here and upsettin' my people and interferin' in my business. Isn't that right, Clara?"

"Yes, suh."

Nothing to hide except sniffin' 'round up there at the camp like a damned ole tomcat. Every time Mistuh Russ turn his back, there was ole Pritchard. Never actually saw him do nothin' but Miss Lucinda look mighty flushed and rumpled a few times. Heard she went back into this here ole stockroom a few times with him when she come to town. What would a pretty woman like that see in a scrawny ole goat like Pritchard?

He was looking at her in a way that made her flesh creep. He was making her so nervous that when he finally spoke she gave a visible start.

"Where did we put that last shipment of insecticide, Clara?"

"I don't know."

"It's in the stockroom. I guess we'd better make an inventory of it before it gets all mixed up. I'll just lock the front door so nobody runs off with anythin' while we're back there."

He slammed the big double door and bolted it. Then he pulled down the curtain that had a sign on it reading, "Back in an hour."

"Come on, Clara."

She felt numb. She walked stiffly, as though her joints hurt. She had always been a little afraid of Mr. Gus, but the fear now was almost paralyzing. She walked ahead of him into the stockroom and Mr. Gus locked that door behind them.

There were no windows in the stockroom. The only light came from a small overhead skylight. It was hot and dark and utterly still in the room. Clara began to tremble like a skittish horse.

"Now, girl, I told you not to do any talkin' to that Miz Waxman, but you done gone and disobeyed me," Pritchard said. "Seems like for your own good I got to teach you a lesson, Clara. Now I don't want to hear a sound out of you. You do any hollerin' and I'm tellin' you now it will go real hard with you."

He had unbuckled his belt and slipped it out of his pants and now he held the brown leather strap loosely in one hand. "Turn around, Clara."

As if hypnotized, she did as he told her, turning so that her back was to him. The urge to scream was bubbling inside her, but at the same time she knew it would not help, that the sound of her voice would be drowned in this hot dusty room among the wooden and cardboard crates and burlap wrapped bales. Directly ahead of her now was a large box painted with checkerboard squares of red and white. On it was the word PURINA. The squares swam dizzily and she had to put out a hand to sustain herself. She felt a trickle of sweat between her naked thighs.

He reached forward to unbutton the back of her dress and pull it away from her shoulders. His motions were slow, methodical, unviolent. His fingers were cold as ice on her back and her skin tried to crawl away from the contact. When he had finished, the honey-colored skin of her soft young back was exposed almost to the swell of her hips.

The blow staggered her. She felt as though she had been split up the middle. But she remained on her feet and no sound came from her clenched lips. A diagonal welt sprang out on the creamy flesh. Pritchard panted like a winded dog. Perhaps it was the sound of that whistling breath that terrified her more than anything else. There was an extreme of passion in it that made her think he really meant to kill her. Rallying the courage that had deserted her until this moment, she turned to face him, holding the dress over her breasts.

It was immediately clear to her that she was wrong in thinking he might be prepared to kill her. Instead of hatred or vengeance, his face wore an expression that was almost beseeching. The belt dropped from his motionless hand.

"Forgive me, Clara."

He went down on his knees and wrapped his arms around her legs and pressed his face against her thighs. She was forced back until she was spread-eagled over the red and white checkerboard box. Clara kept her eyes tightly shut. In a way this was worse than the whipping. She thought if she looked down and saw the top of his head pressed against her she might vomit.

From somewhere, far off, came the long insistent ringing of a phone. The sound of it went on and on. She thought vaguely that someone ought to answer it and she wondered how soon Mr. Gus would let her go.

6

Dan finally put down the receiver. He had been trying for ten minutes to reach Clara Williams at Gus Pritchard's hardware store. It was only after she had hung up that he had realized she might have information of extreme importance for Marty. He had called back almost immediately, but there was no answer. Damned strange. It was, after all, a place of business.

The bell had continued to sound its note of mechanical insistence until at last he had broken the connection and once more began to wonder how Marty and Russ were doing.

CHAPTER FIVE

1

After it was all over, Marty tried to ask herself honestly where she had made her mistake. At what point had the trial slipped away from her and washed a man's life down the drain like a cupful of water? On reflection it was clear to her that she had never had a chance. Judge and jury were dead set against her. Might it have been better to insist on having a woman on the jury? But since women are not called to jury duty in the state of Florida that would have meant taking a volunteer, and it had seemed reasonable to suppose that a volunteer for jury duty must by nature be a busybody.

Perhaps that had been her primary mistake. No, the real mistake was for her to have ever tried to act as defense counsel in the first place. For it had been made perfectly dear to her as soon as the selection of the panel had been completed that they were all against her. She was the outsider, the intruder, the northerner treading on the over-sensitive corns of the South, the woman breathing the solid defenses of a man's world.

Nothing could have made that clearer than the behavior of the judge. The heavy-handed charm he had demonstrated on her visit to his office had disappeared. He regarded her with cold suspicion and dislike which were immediately communicated to the jurors. A colossus in white rayon socks with the obscene belly of a Chinese idol, he had denied her objections, spouted Biblical phrases instead of law, and consistently pretended not to be able to understand her Yankee accent, until at last her voice had lost all conviction even to her own ear. And in the end he had given the jury such a pack of gibberish in his instructions that it had been easy enough for him to compound the confusion already too evident in their minds.

He had done all this with such murderous skill that toward the end of the case her arguments seemed blunted even before they left her lips. Even her mounting anger had not been able to touch him and only once had he permitted himself to say that he hoped the young lady, this very nice-lookin' young lady who had learned her law up there in a New York law school, was not presumin' to instruct this Southern court.

In his instructions to the jury, Judge Grady had stressed reasonable doubt, but he had given them such a cockeyed definition of it that she was still bewildered by the whole thing. It had not only been Russ Perky who had been on trial in that courtroom—Martine Waxman had been tried and convicted as well.

Toward the end it had seemed a nightmare in which she struggled with slow-motion ineffectuality against an overpowering horror. She had felt as she imagined a bull must feel when he first comes out into the ring—out of the cool shadow of the alleyway into the hard glare and the sea of eyes condemning him to death. "I didn't do it," Russ had cried. "I tell you, I didn't do it. You've got the wrong guy."

But the eyes had gazed on him as impersonally as if he were already dead, and the wheels of travestied justice had ground inexorably on.

After that one outburst when the verdict had been

announced, Russ had seemed to shrink inside himself. His pale, boyish face had tightened into a knot and when she had leaned across to him and said, "We'll appeal it, Russ. We'll appeal it and beat them yet," he had not even seemed to hear her.

Later, in telling Dan about it, she had said, "I failed him. I failed him so miserably."

"There wasn't anything you could do about it. That deck was stacked against you from the start."

"But why? Why would they want to do a thing like this to a boy like that? A boy with no record and nothing against him but a lot of talk and suspicion. Why would they toss a man's life on the testimony of a sneaking little rat like that Gus Pritchard?"

"I don't know. What you have to remember is that the human animal can be the cruelest son of a bitch in all history. You turn a mob loose on something defenseless and they can make a weasel in a chicken house look good by contrast."

"But that was no mob. This wasn't done in the heat of passion. It was done coldly and carefully and with plenty of knowledge beforehand. I still believe it was my fault, that without me he would have had a chance."

"Don't go on blaming yourself, Marty. You're not the first lawyer who ever lost a case."

"They hated me, and that was why they convicted him. They hated me because I was an outsider and because I didn't talk their language and because I didn't dress quite the way their women dress and because I talked back to that swine of a judge who hasn't got the least, the remotest idea of what the law is really all about. I tell you Russ would have been better off with any local hack who knew no more about the law than a correspondence course had taught him but who would know how to get down and bootlick those flint-eyed jackals and joke with them and talk their damned language, whatever it is."

"Honey, that's all behind you now. What's the use of giving yourself such a psychological thrashing? You worked hard, and you did the best you could, and it's behind you now. The question is where do you go from here. You'll appeal, of course."

"Absolutely. The first appeal is automatic, anyway. But if for any reason that one fails, then I'll appeal again. If that old water buffalo of a Grady thinks he can get away with this, he's got another think coming.

"But the worst of it is there isn't much time. They're trying to rush this kid into the chair before anyone knows what really happened."

"St. Georgina in a white Plymouth station wagon will stop them."

"You're darned right I will," Marty said feeling that her air of intense conviction was not really fooling anybody.

"The first thing you've got to do is to get hold of that Clara Williams."

"What good would that do? She had already testified for the state."

"That may be, but I suspect she knows a good deal more than she let on."

"What makes you think so?"

"She called here this morning trying to reach you."

"Damn. Didn't she leave any message? Didn't you tell her where to get me?"

"Take it easy. She sounded scared stiff and she hung up in the middle before I could really find out what she was after. Then when I tried to call her back at Pritchard's there was no answer. I would have gone down to find her except that I knew Meg was already on the bus and I had to wait here for her."

"Exactly what did she say?"

"Not much. Just asked for you and then hung up."

"Can you give it to me word for word, Dan? It could be important."

"Like I say, she asked for you and when I told her you weren't here and could I take a message, she said something about it being a bad place to talk and then she hung up. Just before we were cut off she mentioned the name Aunt Bessie."

"Aunt Bessie?"

"That's right. Does it ring a bell with you?"

"Not especially.... Now wait a minute. I think Russ mentioned an Aunt Bessie Carter who lives up there around the camp someplace. I think she's a relative of Clara Williams. He brought up the name when I asked him who might know if there had been any strangers on the lake that day. Then in all the excitement I guess her name got kind of lost in the shuffle. That was after I got so discouraged about Clara Williams. They just won't talk. That's what's so exasperating about it."

"Marty, honey, no Negro in his right mind wants to get mixed up in anything like this that concerns the law and the whites. You've got to remember that the Deep South is still a feudal society in a great many ways, and these people learn to protect themselves the only way they know how—by putting on that Uncle Tom act and pretending not to know nothin' about nobody. You can't really blame them. But why don't you take a chance anyway and go up there tomorrow and see if you can find this woman?"

"I've got to go to Tallahassee tomorrow about the appeal."

"Then I'll play detective for you. I'd like a junket up

to Pelican Bay anyway."

"What about Meg?"

"There's no school tomorrow. Some kind of PTA. meeting. So I'll take her with me. It will be fun for her."

"I don't much like the idea of involving you in all this."

"I'm already involved."

"How so?"

"Someone baptized my tomatoes in kerosene last night," he answered trying to keep his voice as light as possible.

"What are you talking about?"

"Some joker came out here and poured about five gallons of kerosene into the tomato trough. Kerosene and tomatoes do not mix. When you mix them, tomatoes stink of kerosene. Stinking tomatoes not very desirable. Throw stinking tomatoes away."

"You sound as though it were all a big joke."

"I'm not going to cry over it."

"But are you absolutely sure?"

"Any Yankee farmer from New York who can't recognize kerosene had better just pack his traps and head back to Lindy's. But I didn't mention it to start you worrying. It's not so serious."

"I'd say its darned serious if they spoiled your tomatoes."

"Only one tub. Just a gentle warning. If it had been real vandalism, they'd have ruined the entire crop. This was just a polite way of advising the Waxmans to keep their noses clean."

"Now what does that mean?"

"I'll spell it out for you. As far as the good, kind-hearted, simple country folk in this area are concerned, the Perky case is over and finished. They want it dropped. And, more specifically, they don't want you talking to Clara Williams or anyone else about it."

"Why not?"

"For that good question the lady receives a Mercedes-Benz 300 SL and a lifetime supply of paper towels."

"Oh, come off it, Dan. Please be serious."

"The situation, in a nutshell, is like so. We are managing to make ourselves immensely unpopular in this neck of the woods. They never had much love for me in the first place—what with my being an outsider coming down here trying to beat them at their own game with my newfangled notions on scientific farming—but they didn't do anything active about it until you became involved in the Perky case."

"But what has that got to do with it? Why are they so anxious to see Russ Perky dead?"

"I could make a wild guess."

"What would that be?"

"That would be the late lamented Lucinda. My uninformed guess is that the beautiful Mrs. Perky was somehow involved with some of the local gentry. If that was really the case, then they must have been sweating it out like crazy while the trial was on. And it also follows that they must have breathed a big collective sigh of relief when Russ was convicted. If my premise is right, then the last thing they'd want would be someone prying around trying to open the whole thing up again."

"But that's fantastic."

"No more fantastic than a good many other things that go on around here," he said remembering the scene in Lou Tayler's garage.

"But Russ swears Lucinda never cheated on him."

"Do I have to remind you that husbands are always the last to know?"

"And you think Clara knows something about that?"

"People who live out in the country have no secrets. Somebody always has an eye on them. There just is nothing else to do out here. Every time a car goes up the road you want to know who it is and where they're going. With all due respects to you, dear, Lucinda Perky was just about the most seductive looking little piece I ever saw in all my life. Why, she was even on the make for me that time we were up at the camp, and I'm certainly no beauty. Anyway, I'll bet there was plenty of traffic to and from that camp on account of Lucinda, and if that's the case then Clara Williams, or somebody like her, was certainly in a position to get an eyeful."

"Well, my God, if you had that in mind, then why didn't you say something about it before the trial?"

"Because I didn't have it in mind. Or if I did, it was just a shadow that never really materialized. But it was brought home to me pretty forcibly when this kerosene business came along. That's a real nasty stunt and there has to be a real nasty reason for it. I'm well aware that it's kind of a nutty theory, but let's reexamine it. Lucinda Perky was just about the most inflammable bit of goods to ever hit this part of the country. She spent her time hanging around a fishing camp in a pair of the tightest and shortest shorts she could squeeze into. She was seen by a lot of men, and I can guarantee you none of them between the ages of fifteen and ninety ever quite got over it.

"Now what do we know about the lady in question? Not much except that she was hardly what you might call an unplucked flower. She had been married at least twice, worked as a B-girl in some dive in Detroit and picked up a little loose change posing in the nude for sexy magazines. I don't know if she was ever an active, card-carrying prostitute, but I'll bet that at one time or another she wasn't far from it. And there may have been some other juicy chapters in her young life that were even more colorful. Now we take this bundle of joy, this package of clitoral dynamite ..."

"Of what?"

"Never mind. We take this tomato and put her in a place where she's bored stiff and where she generates more excitement than a hurricane, and what happens? She gets bumped off, and the first likely suspect, who also happens to be her husband, is railroaded to the chair in what is probably pretty close to world's record time. And all of a sudden nobody wants to talk about it. Here's a thing with all the juicy ingredients—sex, murder, rape. By rights they should be yapping about it in every barber shop and on every street corner from here to Pahokee. Instead they do as much talking as clams.

"That was the first phase of the battle. Now in phase two you come along and start asking some questions that might be hitting a little close to home. So right away somebody takes it into his head to poison my crop. Or part of it anyway. The thing is that up to this point, hydroponic farming, or Waxman's Folly, has been good for nothing but laughs. Suddenly, however, they are ready to waste several gallons of good kerosene just to let me know how they feel about it. This could be the long arm of coincidence, but if so, it sure has one hell of a reach. I'm more inclined to think that *l'affaire* Lucinda is beginning to worry them."

"Well you certainly seem to have made quite a study of Lucinda. I wonder when you found time to do any farming. Maybe you were part of this flock of panting males that you seem to think were always running up there to the camp just to get a look at her."

"Maybe I was."

"Did you really go to see Lucinda, Dan?"

"Well I did go by there one time to look at a plug casting outfit Russ had up for sale."

"And?"

"He wasn't home."

"Was she?"

"Now to get back to the question of the son of a bitch who attacked my vegetables—"

"You're impossible. Anyway, I have no intention of giving you the satisfaction of being jealous of poor dead Lucinda. So we'll get back to the question of your tomatoes. What do we do now?"

"I know what *I'm* going to do."

"What?"

"I'm going down to Gus Pritchard's hardware store tomorrow and buy me the biggest twelve-gauge shotgun he has in stock. Not, mind you, that I really have any intention of using it. I just want the word to get around. If nothing else, it should give these clowns some pause for thought."

"Do you really think the fact that you buy a shotgun will discourage them?"

"I expect the sale of kerosene in this area to drop off very sharply."

"Let's be serious for a moment."

"What could be more serious than a twelve-gauge shotgun?"

"What I mean is, I wonder if I'm doing the right thing in involving you in this mess. Our whole future is tied up in this farm and you've been sweating over it for a year now. If what you say is so, if my poking around asking questions is creating all this ill will, then I wonder if I have the right to jeopardize all our futures over it."

"So what do you want to do?"

"Maybe I should quit."

"Just put your tail between your legs and slink off in a corner? Is that what you want?"

"No."

"What do you want?"

"I want to go on. I want to save him."

"Then that's what I want for you too. And you will. You must believe that. One way or another, come hell or high water, you will get that boy out of the pokey. I can always grow more tomatoes, but we can't grow a new Russ Perky. You do your job, honey, and let the blooming chips fall where they may."

2

Dan had decided to make the search for Aunt Bessie Carter something of an outing, and as part of this plan he had put Meg in charge of the hard-boiled egg and peanut butter sandwich department. Although at least one egg wound up on the kitchen floor and her sandwiches were somewhat lopsided, the little girl did surprisingly well at it, and it was with an air of pride and confidence that she finally carried the wicker picnic basket out to the car.

"I wish Mommy could come with us," Meg said.

"I do too, honey."

"What is the name of that place you said she went?"

"Tallahassee."

"That's a funny name."

"Well, it's an Indian name. Like Opa-loka or Okeechobee or Weeki-Wachee."

"Oh, Daddy, there isn't really a place named Weeki-Wachee. You're making that up."

"If you think I'm making that up, I'll show it to you

on the map. I can also show you Apalichicola, which sounds like a hulk but isn't, and Choctawhachee Bay and Calooshatchee and Withlacoochee and a couple of others."

"Daddy!" she said with sudden intensity, stopping short and planting her hands on her hips.

"What?"

"You forgot your cigars."

"Did I?"

"I'll run back in and get them. I know just where they are."

When she re-emerged with a handful of cigars he said, "I don't know how I ever got along without you."

"Well since Mommy isn't here, somebody has to look out for you."

"I'm sure you're absolutely right," he answered meekly.

They took the main road out of town and then the cutoff to the lake. As they approached the grassy wall of the dike, he remembered the last time he had come up here. It was the time Russ had not been at home.

Lucinda had come to the door in answer to his knock. She was wearing a yellow silk dressing gown and he had been made immediately aware by the unfettered shape of her breasts and the amount of white skin exposed in the vee of the gown that she was naked under it. The long glance he directed at her half-exposed bosom did not seem to bother her, and she made no effort to cover herself.

The voice had been throaty, the eyes veiled. Carbon copy of the plump blonde who has become the sex symbol of the adolescent male. "It's Mr. Waxman, isn't it?"

"Sure is, honey. Russ around?"

She let her sharp little white teeth slide slowly over

the glistening pink flesh of her lower lip before shaking her head and answering, "Uh-uh."

"Expecting him back soon?"

"You never can tell with Russ. Have you got the time?"

"I've got the time; but who'll hold the horses?" he answered completing the hoary traveling salesman's gag. "Sorry. It's eight-thirty, Mrs. Perky."

"Lucinda."

"Then let's make it Dan."

"Russ won't be back for at least an hour. He left at the crack of dawn to go up to Liberty Point to see how the bass were hitting. Personally, I think he must be nuts. Why any man in his right mind would get out of a warm bed to go fishing is something I'll never understand. Anyway, is there something I can do for you?"

Was it his imagination, or had the yellow silk slipped another inch? Almost the entire, beautifully-rounded globe of her left breast was now revealed, and Dan was beginning to find it a little hard to breathe. His voice sounded choked when he said, "Russ mentioned a plug casting outfit he thought I might be interested in. A South Bend rod and Shakespeare reel, I think."

What a fool he felt like, talking fishing tackle to this astonishing creature with her breasts about to burst out of the yellow silk.

"I wouldn't know one end of a fishing rod from the other," she answered. "But you can come in and wait for him if you like."

It was like that time when he had been about fifteen and had gone down to the Irving Place burlesque just off New York's Union Square. Buying his ticket, he had worn his hat pulled almost down over his eyes, in old-time gangster fashion, for fear that they would turn him away. Then, after the show, he had hung around the stage door waiting for the girls to come out, hoping one of them might smile an invitation to him. He had stood there a long time, a big nervous kid, unhappily aware of his too small suit and too big hands. When at last they came out, he had discovered to his surprise that they were all a good deal older and far less beautiful than they had looked on the stage. It was something of a relief to him when none of them smiled at him and he had been able to go home alone.

"Had your coffee yet?" Lucinda asked.

"Had it early this morning. Before you were even stirring."

"I guess you could always do with another cup. It's only that lousy instant stuff, but if you can stomach it, you're welcome. Come on in."

In his nervousness the words seemed to collide and tumble over each other. "I don't want to intrude on you. Anyway, it's a little later than I thought, and I guess I'd better be getting back. I've got to pick up a sack of nitrates. You tell Russ I'll come by another time."

Her half-smile held a mixture of contempt and lingering invitation. She shrugged her pretty shoulders and said, "Suit yourself."

"Well, I'll be seeing you. So long, Lucinda."

As he walked to the car, he was thinking what a fool he had been. It would have been so easy. There she was practically laying it on the line. She must be absolutely tremendous in bed. Another couple of minutes and that infernal dressing gown would have been off altogether.

Of course, he told himself, you can't go around the neighborhood like some twenty-year-old stud doing this sort of thing to Marty. And it isn't only Marty. There's Meg too. You're supposed to be a happily married man. Are you so impressionable that you get weak in the knees just standing talking to a girl like Lucinda?

Yes, dammit, you are that impressionable. Who wouldn't be? Imagine mild-mannered little Russ Perky spending every night with a thing like that.

By the time he reached the car, the feeling of virtuous renunciation had slipped away and he was ready to face the truth about himself. It had not been marital devotion that had kept him from going into the house with Lucinda. At that moment, the ties that bound him to fidelity had been just about as loose as the sash on that dressing gown.

It had not been that at all. What it had been, plainly and simply, was that Lucinda had been too much woman for him. She had made him feel like a schoolboy. She had just plain scared the hell out of him.

Before switching on the ignition, he briefly considered going back to the house. But even while he thought of it, he knew it was too late. The moment had passed. For better or for worse he would never know now what really lay under that yellow silk.

He never saw her again, and he had even managed to put her pretty much out of his mind until he had picked up the paper that morning three weeks ago and read that she had been murdered.

"This is a funny place, Daddy," Meg said as they passed the camp and drove on along the dusty road toward the cluster of shacks that formed the colored section.

"We were here once before. We went fishing. Don't you remember that?"

"Was it a long time ago? With Mommy?"
"That's right."
"There was a lady with beautiful hair."
"Yes."
"Is she still here?"
"No, not anymore."
"Why not?"
"Well, she's gone away."
"For good?"
"I'm afraid so."
"I'm glad," Meg said with the brutal honesty of childhood.
"Why?"
"I didn't like her."
"Why not?"
"I don't know. I just didn't like her."

He had slowed the car as they passed the camp and in that brief look he could see that in the space of only a few weeks the place had begun to change. The boats and motors were gone—he knew that Marty had arranged to store them at another camp—and the house was shuttered. Rank beds of weeds had already taken possession of the yard. Perhaps it was his own imagination, but he seemed to sense an almost visible aura of tragedy in the shuttered house and abandoned camp. It was as if the world had already written off Russ Perky and the things that had been important to his life.

A quarter of a mile beyond the camp, at a point just before the channel entered the lake, there was a single commercial enterprise—a dilapidated off-brand filling station. Half a dozen Negroes lounged around it in whatever shade they could find. An ancient liver-colored dog opened a disinterested eye at Dan's approach and then closed it again. Heat and inertia lay over the place like blankets.

"Can anybody tell me where to find Aunt Bessie Carter?" Dan asked.

The faces turned toward him, the eyes regarded him with interest, but the mouths remained closed.

"What was that, cap'n?" one of the men finally said.

"I'm looking for a woman named Aunt Bessie Carter," he repeated, patiently.

"You know any Aunt Bessie Carter, Ike?"

Long deliberation followed by slow negative shake of the head.

"You, Pritch?"

"Not me."

"Whut you want with her?"

"Well, I just want to talk to her. I thought she might be le to help a friend of mine who's in trouble."

"You ain't fum the guv'mint?"

"He don't look like he got no summons," one of the onlookers volunteered. "I knows de man wid de summons. Dat's dat mean, ratty lookin' constable."

One of the men, taller, stronger and younger looking than the others, stood up and said in a disgusted voice, "Hell, whut you birds so damn scared about? De man axe you a question and you act like he Hitler. If'n he wants to talk to Aunt Bessie, he gon find her anyhow. Whut he want to say to her is his business. You find her down by the crik, mistuh. She always fishin down dat way near de channel. You cain't miss her. Jus' look for de bigges' woman you ever see."

Dan thanked them and drove on. The dike was now a green wall behind them and the sensation was something like that of driving inside a giant bowl. It was strangely quiet, not even a circling bird in the still air. It was probably something like this, he thought, in '26 when the hurricane hit, except that there had been no dike at that time. On that day the circular winds had scooped the water out of the lake and flung it in a solid sheet over the lowlands on the western shore, thereby virtually wiping out the little town of Moore Haven and drowning more than two thousand people. It was that disaster which had led to the building of the dike and the hurricane gates designed to control the level of the lake. But apart from that, the area of the lake itself had probably changed very little. If anything, it was even more mysterious now with the great wall of the dike shutting it off from the outside world. When you passed the dike going toward the lake and drove down into this flat green quiet, you had the feeling that you had somehow crossed a time barrier to the past.

The shacks were clustered together like a flock of sheep. An old man sat in the doorway of the last one, and Dan got out of the car to ask him how to find Aunt Bessie.

The ancient gaffer sucked on his corncob pipe with toothless gums and gazed at Dan out of bloodshot eyes. "Ain't but one Aunt Bessie roun' here."

"How do I find her?"

"She to de lake fishin'."

"Whereabouts?"

"Back dar," came the vague response.

"Can I get there by car?"

"You got to walk. You jus' follows de shore until you gets to de big trees. You finds her dar."

Dan and Meg parked the car at the end of the road and walked along the carpet of meadow grass. From this vantage point the vast lake, seemingly limitless, stretched before them. Thunderheads, in the ominous shape of mushroom clouds, burgeoned above the eastern shore. Surprisingly, it was a little cooler here, there was a pleasantly moist breeze striking diagonally across the lake. Meg went skipping on ahead.

As they approached the rim of trees, they were no longer on the open shore of the lake. Here the land fronted one of the drainage canals that wound back to the sluice gates. Ahead the canal opened into a channel marked with a row of stakes that stretched away like a flock of long-legged water birds. A woman who looked as big as a hippopotamus sat on the bank holding a cane pole. Her face was hidden beneath the brim of a huge straw hat. Beside her lay half a dozen good sized bass. Dan, acknowledging to himself that he had never been able to catch anything like that, regarded the fish with envy.

"Good morning. Can you tell me where to find Aunt Bessie Carter?"

The hat tilted slowly, exposing a vast round black face shiny with sweat.

"You found her," the fat woman said in a voice as deep as a man's.

"My name is Dan Waxman. This is my little girl Meg."

"Hello, chile."

"Hi," Meg said.

Dan sat down beside her on the grass. She made him feel small. This was the biggest woman he had ever seen; she must weigh close to four hundred pounds.

"The reason I wanted to talk to you, Mrs. Carter ..."

The schoolgirl giggle was disconcerting from so vast a bulk. It rippled her multitude of chins like a dabble of wind across the lake. "Jus' call me Aunt Bessie. Nev' mind that Miz Carter. Never foun' me a man big 'nuff to marry. Always caught me the li'l ole bitty ones and had to throw 'em back."

"All right, we'll make it Aunt Bessie then. I guess you know about the killing over at the Perky place."

She nodded.

"Well I don't believe Mr. Perky killed his wife. I think he was convicted unfairly. I want to try to help him."

"Is that why you come to see me?"

"Yes."

"Whut you 'spect me to do 'bout it?"

"I don't know. I'm not sure. I thought you might know something about it."

"Not me. I don' know nothin'. All I knows is to fish."

"A girl named Clara mentioned your name."

"Clara Williams?"

"Yes."

"She talks too much," the fat woman said flatly, lowering her head so that her face was once more obscured by the giant hat.

Dan felt baffled. There had to be some way to reach this woman, to give her a feeling of confidence.

Suddenly Aunt Bessie looked up at Meg and said, "Here, chile. You wants to hole this fishin' pole?"

Meg's face lit up. "Can I?" she asked.

"Now ain't that whut I'm tellin' you?"

"Is it all right, Daddy?"

"Sure thing, honey."

"But not here," Aunt Bessie said. "The fishin' here ain't so good. Right down there by that big tree," she added pointing to a tree some fifty feet away, "is the bes fishin' they is. You go down by that tree and you sure to catch you somepin'. But don' you let him fool you now. Don' you let him get that ole worm away from you."

"I won't."

"All right then. Scat."

Meg darted off. Aunt Bessie watched her with a careful eye until she was safely established on the bank under the tree. "Hit don' do to talk about killin' in front of a chile."

"Then you do know something," Dan prompted.

"Not me. I don' know nothin'."

"I just thought that since you spend so much time out here fishing, it must be pretty easy for you to keep tabs on people coming and going."

"Oh I sees them all right. I sees everybody comes out of that crik."

"Perhaps you saw someone that day."

"Oh I sees them, but I don' always remember whut I sees. An' if'n I do see somepin', I don' always talk 'bout it neither."

"I wonder why Clara mentioned your name."

"Clara is my sister's chile. She talks too much. Gets herself into a pack of trouble that way. This here is white folk's business. Hit don' pay fo us folks to get mixed up in hit."

He had the feeling that she was playing with him in several different ways. There was, of course, her obvious evasion of the question he had come to ask, and he still had the feeling that she did know something after all. But even apart from that there was a noticeable change, a sort of rhythmic rise and fall in her personality and accent. She was able to spread the Uncle Tom act much more thickly whenever she felt she was getting on to thin ice.

Deciding to change the angle of attack, he said, "Oh well, it's not important. Nice weather we're having anyway."

The cascade of mirth rippled the sea of chins. "Sho' is."

"And the fishing seems to be pretty good."

"Fair 'nuff."

"How about a sandwich?" he asked, indicating the picnic basket.

"I don' mind."

He handed her the basket and she took out one of the sandwiches and began munching on it.

"Now whut was that day you was talkin' 'bout?" she asked, thoughtfully.

"You mean the day of the murder?"

"Mmm."

"The twelfth."

"Now would that be a Monday?"

"Yes."

"Well I don' believe I seen nothin' special that day. Jus' Mistuh Russ."

"What about Mr. Russ?"

"Like you say, it's real nice weather. 'Course it's kinda warm when you big as me."

He understood at last that she would not answer any questions directly. She might tell him what she knew, but it would have to be in her own way, and when it was all over it would be very hard to prove that she had told him anything at all. To hide his impatience he looked over at Meg and said, "Do you think she'll catch anything?"

"She'll get one," the fat woman said with conviction.

The sun inched toward noon. Aunt Bessie munched her sandwich. When she had finished it she wiped her mouth daintily and brushed the crumbs from her lap. "Now you say Monday. I remembers it was mighty hot that day too. Remembers it 'cause I was sittin' right here. Caught me some nice fish that day. Seen Mistuh Russ go out in his boat early that mornin'. Come out of the crik and went on up the lake. Then along 'bout an hour later 'nother boat come out. 'Nother boat from Mr. Russ's camp. This boat actin' mighty peculiar. Actin' like he ain't make up his mine. Ain't doin' no fishin' or nothin', jus' ridin' roun' in circles. He ride aroun' for a li'l ole while and then he turn and head back into the crik lak somepin' after him. Di'n' see him no more. Matter of fac' di'n' see nothin' no more till late in the day when Mistuh Russ come back."

"Do you know who was in that boat, Aunt Bessie?"

"Whut boat?"

"The second boat you saw. The one that you said was acting peculiar and then went back into the creek."

"Might rain," she said looking over at the thunderheads in the west. "Seem lak every afternoon 'bout this time it build up for rain. 'Body sets here on this bank, you can see pretty good on this ole lake. Seen that boat that day an that man whut was in it. Never did see him befo'. Stranger 'roun here. Kine of a solid lookin' man. Square. Wasn't wearin' no hat. Knowed he wasn't from 'roun here cause any man from aroun' here would know better'n to be out in that sun with no hat. He had light-colored hair cause I could see it shinin' in the sun a long way off. Wasn't dressed like no fisherman either. Wearin' a white shirt. You goes to fishin' with a white shirt and them fish sees you a long way off."

Aunt Bessie paused. Dan waited as long as he could, but when no more words seemed forthcoming, he asked, "Could you see how old he was?"

"Seem lak it should be turnin' cooler one of these days. We mos' into November now. Wasn't no ole man. Wasn't no boy neither. 'Bout your age. And he smokin' a ceegar too. I knowed it was a certain kine of ceegar because he throwed it away an it come floatin' in here to the bank. Even kep' the wrapper." She dug into her pocket and took out a little package of waxed paper and unwrapped it and held in her pink palm a faded cigar wrapper on which the name Tampa Nugget was still visible.

"How did you happen to keep it?"

"Nex' day when I heard 'bout what happen to Miz Lucy I come back here and foun' it layin up against the bank. After that, I just kep' it." She took off the hat and fanned herself and said, "Sho' is warm."

"I'm afraid a cigar wrapper won't mean much as evidence. Anyway, it's a pretty popular cigar around here. I smoke them myself. Look here, are you absolutely certain that boat you saw was out of Perky's camp? Don't all the boat liveries around the lake use pretty much the same design of skiff? Couldn't it have been from Slim's or one of the other camps?"

Aunt Bessie took a handkerchief out of her pocket and removed her hat and mopped her shining brow. "Seems like the older a body gets the more you feels the heat. I don' hardly ever recall it bein' so warm for this time of year. Now if there's one thing ole Aunt Bessie don' need, it's somebody tellin' her what these here fish boats on this lake look like. I bin watchin' boats come and go here for better'n thirty years. Mistuh Russ, he got him a red number on all his boats. That boat had a red number on it. I could see it as plain as I see you."

"The police checked over his rental lists for that day and there was no record of any boat being taken out."

"Mistuh man, if you got so much confidence in the police, wherefore is you sittin' here talkin' to me?" the fat woman asked shrewdly.

Dan grinned at her and said, "I guess you're right. Anyway, you're certain the man was a stranger?"

"Stranger to me. I knows 'em all what comes up here to the lake. Ole Mistuh Gus Pritchard. Ole Mistuh Judge Grady. Ole Mistuh Lou Tayler from the garage. All of 'em."

"Did you say Judge Grady?"

"Sho'."

"He came up here?"

"Every couple of weeks."

"You mean before the murder?"

"Ain't I jus' finished tellin' you that?"

"Was he by any chance a friend of Mrs. Perky's?"

"Use to become the end of the hurricane time we gets us a northwester to cool things off. But not this year. No sir. Sho' he was her friend. Seem like every man who ever see that chile was her friend." Suddenly, as if afraid of having committed herself too far, she heaved her vast bulk upwards and said, "I can't sit round here no more talkin' 'bout the weather with you, mistuh. I got me things to do."

"All right," Dan said, grateful for at least having gotten that much information from her. "Come on, Meg."

"Wait, Daddy. Wait a minute. I think I'm getting a bite."

The tip of the cane pole quivered.

"Hit him," Aunt Bessie grunted.

The pole bent into an arc. Meg screamed. Out of the water, mailed coat gleaming, came a monster of a bass. He tried to climb into the sky and, failing to reach it, fell back into his natural element with a might splash. Meg screamed again. Dan was about to reach for the pole when Aunt Bessie laid a restraining hand on his arm and said, "Leave that chile alone. It's her fish. She got to land it or lose it herself. Don' you touch that pole."

Dan drew back and stood watching while Meg battled the big bass. For a moment he thought the fish might draw the little girl down into the water, but when he made a movement toward her the fat woman shook her head again in warning.

Ten minutes later it was over. The fish lay flopping on the bank and Meg danced around him whooping with excitement. Aunt Bessie unhooked the fish and smacked him over a projecting tree root. After that she took the now defunct bass and wrapped him in a double sheet of newspaper and handed him to Meg.

The little girl's eyes were still starry with excitement. "Is he really mine?"

"You cotched him?"

"Yes."

"Then he's yours. Ain't nobody else's. You take him home and eat him. Be sure you skin him good, mistuh."

"I will," Dan answered. "And thanks for everything."

"I ain't done nothin' for you. We done talk 'bout the weather, is all. You jus' remember that now. Us folks down here inside the dike livin' on guv'mint land. We don't want ole judge Grady sniffin' round us. You jus' remember that, mistuh. Nobody down here knows nothin' 'bout nobody. And we wants to keep it that way."

CHAPTER SIX

1

Marty drove east and south from the state capitol to the prison. She passed innumerable orange juice stands, monkey jungles, reptile institutes, aquariums, parrot jungles and Indian villages, all strategically placed along the highway to catch the fleeting tourist buck. At Starke she turned north again toward Raiford and the state prison.

The prison walls hung long and low on the horizon. They looked as ominous as thunderclouds. Even the peaceful rural scene surrounding them, prisoners working in the fields, cattle grazing contentedly, did little to alleviate the grimness of those towers and ramparts.

She parked the car in front of the administration building and checked in at the main gate. There she was told to wait for an escort. When he arrived—a young guard wearing one of the tan uniforms that were manufactured in the prison clothing shop—she was passed through the electronic detector. Even after she had emptied her purse of everything metallic the machine still buzzed angrily. Only after she had removed her wrist watch would it let her through.

"Hello, Mrs. Waxman," the guard said. "My name is Parker."

"How did you know me?"

"Russ told me about you. We figured you'd be here today."

Parker was a squarish, sandy-haired man with a strong, intelligent face. He bore little resemblance to her conception of the average southern jailer. There was something disturbingly familiar about him and it took her a moment to place him. Suddenly she remembered where she had seen him—at Lucinda's funeral—the stocky, square-jawed man standing bareheaded in the rain. She could almost swear that this was the same man.

"How did you make out with the appeal?" Parker asked.

"Not so good."

"They turned you down?"

"Yes."

"I'm sorry to hear that."

This was surprising talk for a guard. If he was hostile toward the prisoner, he certainly did not show it.

"I based the appeal on the fact that the judge's instructions were contrary to law and exceeded his function, but the court decided against me.

"You could sum it all up in one sentence. All the weeks of preparation, the hours of talk. They decided against me."

"Russ was really sweating it out last night."

"I know. I can hardly bring myself to tell him."

"Do you want me to do it?" the guard asked.

"That's decent of you, but the responsibility is mine, and I'll just have to face up to it. You seem—quite concerned about him."

"Does that surprise you?"

"I guess it does. I should think that to be a guard here you would have to get very callous about this sort of thing."

"Does a doctor get callous when he has to tell a mother her child is dying of leukemia? You never get callous about men in the death house."

"I had the feeling that you might have known him."

"You mean before?"

"Yes."

"No," Parker said. "I never knew him."

They had emerged on to the shaded walk where the prison band was playing the *River Kwai* marching song with more spirit than skill. The sprightly music floated across the sun-dazzled ball field. A long line of prisoners in faded blue uniforms stood marching in time to the music in front of the dining hall.

A marching song for men with no place to go, Marty

thought. Is it the extra needle or coincidence? She was aware of cold eyes following her, of whispers. Suddenly she was immensely conscious because of the hungry stares on her breasts and watching the movement of her hips under the black silk. She tried to hold herself as straight as possible.

"We'll have to take the long way around," Parker said. "They're putting in a new road out back of the Rock and the place is covered with mud."

She was grateful for even this small delay before having to face Russ.

Behind the courtyard was the old building they called the Rock. Here were located the punishment cells for intractables. She was able to peer briefly into one of the cells as they passed by. Seen through the barred six-inch square in the door which was the sole opening for light and air, the interior of the cell was a frightening sight. Six men squatted like animals in the gloom on the stone floor. There was no furniture of any kind, only the open pit of a stone toilet. Originally, Parker explained to her, regular toilets had been installed in the cells, but these had later been removed since men had literally torn them off their fixtures and tried to beat each other to death with them.

Beyond the Rock was the clothing factory. Here were congregated the known homosexuals. The practice was to keep them together as much as possible so as not to allow them to corrupt the others. But these precautions were largely useless. Few of the younger men, unless they were exceptionally strong and able, had much chance to escape them. Sooner or later, one of the old pros would corner him. Then came the desperate, soundless struggle in the night. For if he screamed for help or cried out to one of the guards, he would be a dead man. Next day he would be found with his throat or belly slit. Homosexual rape, Parker explained, was perhaps the biggest individual problem in prison life. Thus far no one had found a way to prevent it. You might, if you had time and space, cut it down somewhat, but in the overcrowded conditions that prevailed in most prisons there was no way to avoid it.

Beyond the clothing shop was the tobacco factory. Here was manufactured the tobacco that was distributed in small quantities to the prisoners. Marty was aware of clouds of bittersweet tobacco dust and the clank of machinery and the little orange bags of snuff that looked as strong and black as swamp water. Again, veiled, reproachful eyes followed her with quickened interest and then were suddenly averted by the sight of the guard beside her.

Bemused by the sun and the pressure of what still lay before her, Marty had an impression of unreality, of past and present merging. Scattered impressions filtered through.

The band music, now far away, but still sprightly; a burly Negro with one leg off at the knee, hops across the ball field; in a fenced-off sector another prisoner has set up a crude workshop where he repairs toys and bicycles which will later be distributed to children through charitable organizations. From bits and pieces of various defunct vehicles he has put together a cleverly made motorcycle which he has painted a flaming red. The bike, Parker tells her, can do over forty miles an hour. But of course it will never go anywhere. The builder is in for 199 years.

Beyond the other buildings, surrounded by a private complex of walls and wire, stands the somber, brooding death house. It is a small, square, flat-topped structure.

They pause at the great iron gate while Parker presses a button. Cold, incurious eyes peer down at them from behind the bulletproof glass of the watchtower. The electrically powered gate swings slowly back. As they pass through, it clangs shut behind them.

Beyond the wall and the building is an empty courtyard. The air in here is motionless, stifling. No sounds from the outside world are heard. It is like entering a tomb, except here death stands waiting just outside.

Parker presses another button and a small door opens and they pass into the darkness and the comparative coolness of the office. The man in charge glances up from his magazine and nods to Parker. Marty enters the narrow corridor before the cells.

Twelve cells. Ten of them occupied. In them, in the order of their execution dates, are the men who must die. Those who are closest to the small green door at the end will go first.

These are big, comfortable cells, as befit these men who are the elite of prison life. For around this small, grim building, the rest of the prison seems to revolve. The grapevine is live with gossip concerning the men in these cells. As they approach their final day, their every move is watched and reported. The faces of these doomed men are studied almost with reverence. It is as if, standing on the threshold, they already possess some secret, unknown to the rest of us.

Russ's pale, narrow face appears between the bars. He summons a wan smile for her. It is apparent that he has lost a good deal of weight. Hollows have replaced the boyishly-rounded cheeks. His gaunt face looks many years older. She has the frightening impression that she is looking, not at a living man, but at a death's head.

He is so anxious to ask her about the appeal and she is so reluctant to tell him that for a moment neither can speak. Wordlessly she hands him the packet of stamps she has brought. She has selected them upon the advice of a dealer—a two-cent Italian East Africa, an eight-cent Cuban Maximo Gomez, a penny Liberian, Correos del Peru, Helvetia, Cote D'Ivoire, and many others.

He takes them in a lifeless hand. They bring no spark of interest to his eyes. Of what importance can stamps be to him now? The unasked question is framed on his lips.

"I have some bad news, Russ," she said in a strained voice.

She waited for him to say something, but he only stared at her.

"I'm afraid they've turned the first appeal," she went on. "Of course we can appeal again and I have already filed to that effect. Sooner or later they must realize what a farce that trial was. I am hoping that it will only be a matter of days until the second appeal is heard and I have absolute confidence that the original verdict will be thrown out on grounds of prejudice. You've got to keep believing in that, Russ, and you've got to try to hold on."

Even to her own ears her words sound hollow, lacking in conviction.

Suddenly, from the adjoining cell, a heavy voice says, "Fug 'em all, kid. Spit in their goddam eyes."

Russ has managed to find his voice, although it is little more than a croak. "That's my friend Mack. Mack Farr."

She is familiar with the name. It has been made quite famous in the past few weeks. Mack Farr is a

Korean war hero who has killed a policeman during an attempted holdup. The question of special dispensation for him because of his war record arose several times during his trial, but in the end, the jury decided that regardless of any special services he may have rendered his country in the past, he must still pay the penalty for his crime. He is slated to die one week after Russ.

"Hi," he says cheerfully. "Shake hands."

He puts his hand between the bars and she gives him hers. He is a fair-haired man with bright blue eyes set under heavy brows. His face is not unlike Parker's. They might be brothers. There, Marty thinks, but for the grace of God....

"You're the prettiest goddam lawyer I ever saw. Some guys have all the luck."

His hand is like a vise. He squeezes her fingers. She tries to withdraw but he will not release her. The sensation of power in his hand is so immense that she can feel herself growing dizzy and weak, not only from the pressure he is bringing to bear on her hand, but also from the contact of his brutal male flesh against her own.

"All right, Farr, cut it out," Parker says.

But Farr will not release her. She has made no sound, but she is in very real pain. Tears form in her eyes. Parker steps forward to grip the convict's wrist. Farr releases her and she stumbles away from him. Her legs are like jelly. He has frightened her more than she will admit.

By a major effort of will she stiffens her spine and moves back to Russ. He has watched the little scene in front of Farr's cell without any evidence of interest.

"I'm going back to Tallahassee tomorrow, Russ, and I'll file an appeal before the Supreme Court. I have every confidence...."

Her voice falters. She really has no confidence at all. No confidence in anything anymore. Not in herself, nor the law, nor justice, nor the milk of human kindness.

"I have every confidence that the appeal will be upheld. But if for any reason it should fail, there is still the governor. That gives us two perfectly good chances, Russ, and one of them is bound to succeed."

She waits for some word from him, but his lips remain closed. When she asks, "Do you need more reading matter? Cigarettes? Stamps?" he only shakes his head in reply.

Suddenly he gives her a bewildering smile. It is a smile of resignation, of relief. She can see what is happening to him. The shadow of death has already touched him. Now that the appeal has been rejected, he will no longer hope. He will no longer fight. He cannot be disappointed again because he will not hope again. It is as though he were hypnotized by the prospect of his own fate.

Since he will not speak and since there seems nothing more to say, she prepares to leave. "I'll be back as soon as possible, Russ, and next time with better news."

Parker guides her out.

Farr whistles maliciously at her as she passes his cell.

2

"The thing is I just don't give a sheet," Farr said.

"I guess I don't either anymore," Russ answered.

They were sitting with their faces pressed against the bars of their cells, talking softly. They could not see each other, but that did not matter; in their loneliness there was enough companionship in a voice.

"Why did you squeeze her hand?" Russ asked.

"Why not? It's the last time I'll ever touch a woman. I wanted to make the most of it."

"You hurt her."

"She'll recover. What the hell is she doing in a business like this anyway? You can see how much good she's done you."

"Yeah."

"Although it's probably not her fault. When society decides to lower the boom on you, kid, you've had it. Guilty or not."

"I'm not guilty."

"Well I am. I killed the son of a bitch and I make no bones about it. In a way, we're all guilty as hell."

"How do you mean?"

"Ever read any poetry?"

"Not since I was in school, and I don't remember any of what I read there."

"You ever hear of a guy named Oscar Wilde?"

"No."

"He was an Englishman. A fag. He served some time himself. Anyway he wrote a thing called "The Ballad of Reading Gaol" and there are a couple of lines in it that go like this:

> Yet each man kills the thing he loves,
> By each let this be heard,
> Some do it with a bitter look,
> Some with a flattering word,
> The coward does it with a kiss,
> The brave man with a sword!

"That was the last good thing he wrote. When he got

out he was never any good again."

"You sure have had a lot of education, haven't you, Mack?"

"The best. Three years at U.C.L.A. before I decided the hell with it."

"That's why I can't understand how you wound up in a place like this."

"Education doesn't have much to do with it. It's a matter of basic philosophy. Whether you'll take all the crap from society or you won't. Like I said, my philosophy is a very simple one. I plain just don't give a sheet. I didn't even have to kill that half-assed cop. I had taken his gun away from him and I could just as easily have clubbed him over the head and left him there. But after I hit him and he fell down, something happened to me. I wanted to kill him. I remember I kept thinking, what the hell? What the hell? So I shot him twice right in the head. You ever shoot a man in the head, Russ?"

"I never shot anybody any place."

"You know what it sounds like? It sounds like you busted a melon with a bat."

"Didn't you feel anything when you killed him?"

"The truth is, kid, the only thing I felt was pretty good. The fact that there was one less silly old fart in the world sure didn't bother me. Just remember I had a year in Korea with the First Marine Division. We had the worst of it—the retreat from the Chosin reservoir after the Chinese came in. That was a nice little war. Harry Truman's private little war. The war that licked the recession and raised the Dow Jones stock average. Anyway I got used to killing. I don't know how many guys I killed there. I killed with a .45 and with a bayonet and with a BAR and one son of a bitch I killed with my hands. I got him by the throat and I held on till his fugging eyeballs fell out of his fugging head. Now why did I kill him? Can you tell me that?"

"Because you were in a war."

"You mean that I really believed that crap that I was protecting the world for the United Nations? Nuts. Or that I killed because I was told to kill? You think all I needed was some old windbag of a general with dyed hair to say, 'Mack, my boy, you get out there and kill. Kill every motherfugging son of a bitch you see. And when you come back, if you come back, that old bastard Syngman Rhee will give you a nice, shiny little medal.' Hell no. I killed for the same reason you killed your wife."

"I didn't kill her," Russ said mechanically.

"Anyway, I killed because I wanted to. Because I got so I liked it. Because the natural function of a man is to kill and when you deny him that you make a pansy out of him. And after they showed me how to do it and told me it was okay, how was I supposed to wind up? Spend the rest of my life selling life insurance and brown-nosing some son of a bitch in an office? It's like those two blacks down the line near the door. You know what they're in for don't you?"

"I heard they killed a man in the Rock."

"But did you hear how they did it? Or why they did it?"

"No."

"They got into a little trouble with one of the guards so they were in a punishment cell on bread and water. Well after a while they took a kind of poor view of that so one day—I love this—they decided to kill the next son of a bitch that was put in with them. Not for any special reason, just for the plain, downright hell of it. So they swiped a spoon and sharpened it on the floor till they had a pretty good edge on it and the next guy that was put in with them they stuffed a shirt in his goddamned mouth so he couldn't holler and then they sat down to cut his head off with that goddamned spoon. The good part of it is they didn't even know him. Never saw him before in their goddamned lives.

"Anyway, they finally got the head off. And I guess it took them all night. You try to cut a guy's head off with a spoon some time. Anyway, they got the head off and then they started pounding it on the floor. And they kept on pounding it till all the bones were broken and they could squeeze it up real narrow and push it between the bars.

"And in the morning when the guard come along—for all I know it was that mealy-mouthed Parker—there was the goddamned head lying in the corridor looking up at him. Now I think these two birds are really great men."

"What's the matter with you? They must be nuts."

"Well, that was their defense at the trial. Naturally they said they were out of their heads from a starvation diet of bread and water. But the doctors didn't go along with that. They gave them a whole series of tests and then said that in their opinion there was nothing wrong with them except that they just didn't give a good goddam. So they stood trial and here they are."

There was a long silence between them. Night ticked away in the square stone house. Life ticked away. In their cells the two Negroes who would die in the morning slept as if there were no tomorrow.

Farr's sardonic laughter floated between the bars and his deep voice said, "What's the matter, kid? Did I shock you?"

"I guess I just never thought of it your way."

"Did you ever do any hunting?"

"Some."

"What kind?"

"Rabbits. Quail. Sometimes deer. I used to go with a gang from the plant."

"Why?"

"You mean why did I go hunting?"

"That's right."

"I don't know. I guess I enjoyed it."

"But what was it you enjoyed most about it?"

"I guess being out in the fresh air. The exercise. Camping out. All that sort of thing."

"Bull. If that was all there was to it, you could have just as much fun taking a walk around the block or going on a picnic. I'll tell you why you got such a bang out of it. What you really enjoyed was the act of killing. The taking of life is a fundamental instinct that has to be satisfied. It stands to reason that you don't go hunting just for the meat. Hell, it would be a lot cheaper and easier to just buy a pork chop in the butcher shop. What every man needs, what you get out of hunting, is the excitement, the sense of power. Maybe, in a funny kind of way, there's a Freudian explanation for it. What I mean is that we get the same kick out of it that we get out of a brand-new shiny broad. Only it's better because it's absolutely fundamental and goes all the way back to the cave and the stone ax. Don't think the judge and the jury weren't getting it, too, when they lowered the boom on you.

"They all get their gun over it one way or the other, even to the nice little law-abiding son of a bitch who only reads about it in the papers. I tell you they're all standing by with their hands on their pants ready to snap to attention. I know it, and I know the charge they get out of it, and that's why I can spit in their goddamned eyes and die laughing."

Now that Farr had boldly mentioned their close proximity to death, now that it was out in the open, Russ felt a surge of panic-ridden fear as if he had been plunged into black swamp water and felt something slimy and elemental rub against him.

"Ain't you afraid, Mack! Ain't you just putting on an act?"

"Afraid of what?"

"Of that—thing in there." He could not bring himself to name it.

"Sheet no. I'd be more afraid of going to the dentist. I know that hurts more and takes longer. Don't even think about it, kid. One lousy minute and it's over. Life is all a crock anyway. What difference does a few lousy years make? And they don't give you any guarantees anyway. Maybe you get hit by a truck or struck by lightning or have your guts rot away with cancer. What the hell."

Farr had a knack for administering this sort of rough comfort. He somehow managed to minimize the importance of life so that death seemed no more than putting a period at the end of damned silly farce.

Suddenly, surprisingly, his deep voice quoted: "'By my troth I care not: a man can die but once; we owe God a death ... and let it go which way it will, he that dies this year is quit for the next.'"

Russ did not speak.

Finally Farr said, "That's about the best thing that was ever written about it, kid. That pretty well sums it up. But if it still bothers you, don't think about it. Think about what a gorgeous piece Lucinda was."

"How do you know that?" Russ asked stiffly, feeling

the old hackles of jealousy rise again.

"How do I know what?"

"About Lucinda."

Farr chuckled. "Why I guess you told me. Didn't you?"

"No, I never told you."

"Then maybe somebody else did."

"What do you mean somebody else did? You been here in jail the same as me. Nobody could have told you nothing about my wife. I want to know how you knew her name or what she looked like."

"Maybe I knew her."

"Knew her where?"

"Before you. In Detroit."

"Then why didn't you say something about it?" Russ asked in a surly voice.

"Why should I? It didn't seem important."

"Well it's goddamned important to me."

"What difference does it make now? She'd dead, isn't she?"

"How well did you know her?"

"Well enough."

"What does that mean?"

"Just what it sounds like."

"You're a goddamned liar."

"Am I? Then I'll tell you a little bit about her," Farr said with brutal emphasis. "She had a mole high up on her right arm just below the point of the shoulder. And she had an appendix scar on her belly. And there was a little scar on the side of her forehead, too, where she had cracked up one time in a car smash. That was why she wore her hair long on that side. You want to hear more?"

"No," Russ grated.

"Why get in such a stew? Whatever happened

between me and Lucinda wasn't on your time anyway. And that's one nice thing about quiff; it doesn't wear out with use. Regardless of what she gave me, there was still plenty left for you."

"Shut up! Shut up, goddamn you!"

"I been laughing about it for days," Farr went on in a casual tone. "Two guys who knew the same broad, and one of them her husband, meet up side by side in the death house. Now if that isn't one for the books."

"I told you to shut up," Russ bellowed. "If I could get my hands on you I'd—"

"You'd what, dearie?" Farr asked in mocking tones.

Russ was cursing incoherently. His face was contorted in a mask of viciousness. The guards came running. As soon as Russ saw the men in uniform a change came over him. He shut his mouth. As if his rage had evaporated in one burst, he went back to his cot and sat down. His face resumed its smooth, youthful look. The only sound in the cells was Farr's soft laughter.

3

There is silence now. Silence and darkness. Those who can sleep do so. The others wait, alone with their thoughts. There is no tick of clock or watch. Although these men in the death house are so vitally concerned with the passage of time, they have no way of measuring it except by the rise and fall of the sun. Somewhere in the dark a man breaks wind loudly while someone else curses softly.

In the outer office the guard dozes in his chair. The magazine has slipped between his legs and the faint pressure on his groin has given him an erotic dream. He stirs in the chair as his hands grope for breasts more beautiful than any he has ever known. He sighs heavily in his sleep.

But a quarter of a mile away in the foul, old building called the Rock it is not so quiet. There men talk the long night away because, to them, the night is as meaningless as the day.

"They takin' them two out tomorrow."

"How you know that, man?"

"The word, man. The word."

"What time they go?"

"Maybe ten. Maybe eleven. Warden don't want to miss his lunch."

"Ole warden, he eat pretty good."

"Chicken, man. Sometimes turkey. Roast beef. Grits. Gravy."

"Knock that off, you son of a bitch. You drivin' me crazy wid dat talk."

"Trouble wid you, man, you eats you bread too fas'. That why you gets so hongry. This your first time in ole Rock, man?"

"Yeah, man."

"This is my fifth time. Five times in ole fuggin' Rock. Firs' time I was jus' like you. Gobble dat bread an water down an' then starve. Now I knows better. Now I takes me a long long time about it. Firs' I sets it down on de flo' and jus' looks at it. I stare at it until it seems like I can't hardly stand it no mo'. Seems like I'm gonna blow apart. Then I starts. But not wid de bread. You got to keep de bread for las'. Firs' you drinks all de water. Dat bloats you. Fills your gut. Takes de edge off de honger. Den you breaks off a li'l piece of bread an' mouths it real slow. You got to make every crumb seem lak it four times as big. Dat way, by de time you finish, you eaten you a meal."

"Shut you' hole, dog boy."

"Who you callin' dog boy?"

"Ain't you de dog boy?"

"Never been no dog boy in my whole life, an' you knows it."

"Heard you de dog boy at de road camp."

"You knows dey don't put no dog boy in heah. Ole dog boy got to live by hisself, else he be dead in about half a minute."

They are referring to the prisoners who are trained to handle the hounds that are used to track escapees. No men in prison life are hated and despised as much as these dog boys.

But the argument that might have blossomed into a fight slowly dies away. No one really cares. Heads slump forward onto chests and hardly anyone hears what is going on in the tier above where two old cons have cornered a nineteen-year-old. The boy has been sent up for stealing two truck tires. He has slender good looks and curly black hair. One of the men holds a knife at his throat while the other paws at his clothing. The boy's eyes are wide with terror. Black horror crawls through his soul like a great spider. The scream that tears through his throat is caught between clenched teeth and is only a bubble against the edge of the night.

The prison sleeps now, but in his quarters on the edge of the compound Ben Parker, the guard who has been Marty's escort, is still awake. He lies in bed talking in whispers to his wife. Moonlight etches the room in silver. The walls are thin and two children sleep in the adjoining room. Parker is restless.

"Why don't you try to sleep, Ben?"

"I have tried, honey. I just can't seem to make it."

"Are you worried about something?"

"Nothing special."

"Is it the execution tomorrow? Does it upset you?"

"A little."

"Do you have to be there?"

"I guess I do. The only way to get out of it would be to go to the super and beg off. I don't want to do that."

"Would he consider it so terrible?"

"Maybe not, but it would certainly put me in a funny light. He might begin to think I was in the wrong line of work."

"And he might be right."

"We've been over all this before, Marge. Let's not start again."

"It just seems like such a waste."

"Of me?"

"Yes."

"But I feel something for these men. I know that some of them—a guy like Farr for instance—would think no more of killing me than he would of squashing a fly, but there are a great many more who are really decent enough kids and who need help in the worst way. They need somebody to talk and to do small favors for them. Even if it's just the tone of voice in which you talk to them, it can mean the difference between being made to feel like a man or an animal. That's what I try to do for them."

He did not go on with it. This sort of solemn talk about the rights of prisoners always made him feel like a fool. What could outsiders know? And even though Marge lived on the prison grounds, she was still an outsider. To her the prisoners were not personalities; they were simply animated blue uniforms seen from a distance. She could not be expected to understand what it was really like to be inside with them, any more than she could understand what it would really be like in that room tomorrow, watching the body of a dead man lashing against the straps that held him to the chair and smelling the stink of his burning flesh.

Yet was it really this, he asked himself, that was keeping him awake, or was it the knowledge that Martine Waxman had recognized him as the man she had seen at Lucinda's grave? He had known her immediately as the woman he had seen standing a little way back from the rest of them on that rainy day when they had buried Lucinda. To have her then turn up at the prison as Perky's lawyer had come as a shock. It was one of those things he could never have anticipated. He had, he thought, managed to conceal his surprise pretty well. And for a moment, he had imagined that she might not recognize him; but then he had seen the little spark of knowledge suddenly flare in her eyes. She had covered it up, of course, but there was no doubt in his mind that she had recognized him.

Worried, restless, he stirred again, and Marge turned and put her arm across him and held his head against the hollow of her throat. He felt the slow surge of warmth in his loins. She reached up and slipped the lace strap of nightgown from her shoulder. His mouth covered the point of her breast. Her small warm hand found its accustomed place between his legs. The nightgown was rolled up around her hips. He kicked the sheet off and moved toward the moment of forgetfulness.

CHAPTER SEVEN

"You look absolutely shattered," Dan said.

Marty slumped down in the wicker chair on the screened porch and said, "I am."

"You're doing too much. Too much driving. Too much running around."

"How can I do too much when there's so little time left? Anyway, it's not the doing that hurts; it's the realization that nothing I do does any good. I tell you, I just don't understand it. Why should the State Supreme Court refuse a hearing on a capital offense where a man's life is at stake? It's incredible. They won't even talk to me. I quote law to them by the hour, and they stare back as if I were talking Greek."

"As far as they're concerned, you probably are. Apparently this thing is really a political hot potato."

"Don't tell me Grady and that infernal prosecutor influence the Supreme Court too?"

"Why not?"

"I don't know," she answered wearily. "I don't know that much about state politics. I just have the feeling now that they're passing the buck along to the governor. Since he can't repeat himself in office anyway, I guess they figure they might as well let him carry the load. But what I really don't understand is if it's really Grady who's putting the pressure on in this thing, and apparently it is, why should it mean so much to him? Why should he be so bound and determined to hang Russ?"

"I can give you the answer to that easily enough. It came out in my talk with Aunt Bessie."

She tapped her palm against her forehead and said,

"I've been in such a fog of disappointment I entirely forgot to ask you about that. You found her all right?"

"Yes, I found her. We had quite a conversation about the weather and fishing and various other matters. Did you know that Grady spent a lot of time at the Perky camp? And that apparently he went there for something else besides fishing?"

"You're kidding."

"I've never been more serious."

"But good Lord, that's all we need. Don't you see that we have grounds for a mistrial if we can show that the judge was prejudiced?"

"Sure, but can you show it?"

"Well, what you're telling me would certainly seem to indicate it."

"Only if you can prove it. Let's assume that you confront him with it and that he denies it. Where do you go from there? You'd have to have sworn testimony from witnesses, and where do you find them? The Negroes are much too frightened of Grady to ever testify against him, and even if they did, who would believe them? As for the rest of the local folk who might know something about it, they seem to be in a real conspiracy of silence. Anyway, there may be nothing to it; it's just the opinion of an old colored mammy who may, for all I know, have imagined most of it."

"What I don't understand is why Grady didn't disqualify himself."

"I would think because he wanted the whole thing kept under strict control where he could see just which way the investigation was heading and then steer it away from any presumably dangerous ground."

"Wait a minute, Dan. Are you seriously suggesting that Grady killed Lucinda? What would be the point in it? From the position of the body, she was obviously killed while resisting an attacker. Since your theory is that Grady was having her anyway, why should she resist him?"

"Could be she was blackmailing him."

She shook her head. "That may be, but I know for a fact that Judge Grady was in Tallahassee at a statewide political meeting the day Lucinda was killed. He was there the entire day, and he's got fifty witnesses to prove it."

"How did you happen to check on that? Don't tell me you had a hunch along these lines too."

"Just a sneaking suspicion. There had to be some explanation for his conduct at the trial, and so I thought I'd run a sort of routine check on him. But you mentioned Pritchard and Tayler. What about them?"

"And what about maybe a dozen others? Where would we start in the time we have left? Anyway, why would they have raped her? My theory is that all the boys were getting it anyway," Dan said shrugging his shoulders in a gesture of confusion.

"You're forgetting that Russ has already admitted the rape part. Unless—now wait a minute. Just say that again. I mean about Pritchard and Tayler."

"I said why should Pritchard or Tayler have raped her since it's my hunch that they were getting what they wanted anyway?"

"But what made you say that when you already knew that Russ had raped her?" Marty asked.

"I guess I'm just not too bright."

"No, there's more to it than that. Something in the back of your mind. Are you thinking the same thing I am?"

"I don't know, sweetie. What are you thinking?"

"That she was raped twice that day."

"I should think that even for Lucinda that would have been some kind of a record."

"But wait a minute. Look at it this way. It was principally Russ's admission of the rape that was so damaging to the defense. And that was certainly why the appeal was denied. They decided if he was capable of raping her, then he was certainly capable of killing her. That, besides that swine Grady, was what really convicted him. But if we could prove she was raped twice—the second time by a party or parties unknown—it would change everything."

"And without witnesses how do you prove it?" Dan asked.

"Isn't there some medical way?"

"Let's be more specific. What?"

"I'd have to ask a doctor about it, but there must be some difference in the semen."

Dan grinned at her and said, "I was wondering how long it would take you to get around to it. The same thought occurred to me this morning, and I've already checked with John Engel on it. To begin with, Lucinda is dead and buried and no examination of her body now would prove anything at all. Too much time has elapsed. Even if some remnants of the discharge still remained, the sperm would, of course, be long since dead, and there would be no way of establishing its origin. Engel says that even if you got it fresh, it would still be a very chancy matter, and that this way it's absolutely out of the question.

"Still, even if it's only an assumption," he went on, "it's a pretty fair assumption at that, and if you follow along those lines, it ties in with something else I learned today. Something Aunt Bessie mentioned between comments on the cloud formation. Namely that there was a second man around the camp that day. He was seen."

"By whom?"

"By Aunt Bessie. Apparently there is very little that goes on around there that she isn't up on. Anyway, she spotted Russ going out fishing early that morning and then coming back again in the afternoon. None of this, incidentally, will she swear to. But she also says that she saw another man out on the water in one of Russ's boats. She doesn't know the exact time, because she doesn't carry a watch, but she's sure it was some time after noon because her stomach was talking to her. Anyway, this lad was a stocky, fair-haired man in a white shirt and not wearing a hat. He seemed indecisive on the water, only staying out a few minutes and then turning around and going back up the channel in the direction of the camp. Her final piece of evidence is that he smoked Tampa Nugget cigars."

"A stocky, fair-haired man who smokes cigars. The latest census shows 38,000 stocky, fair-haired men in Okeechobee County who smoke cigars. And even if we could find him, we still don't know that he had anything to do with the crime," Marty said.

"Honey, this is the time when you clutch at straws. If what Aunt Bessie says is true, then there was a man at the camp that morning when Lucinda was alone there. Obviously, if he used one of their boats, he came to the camp to get it. Then he took the boat out on the lake, but only stayed out a few minutes before turning around and going back to the camp. Then let's carry the assumption a little further. He went back to the camp with something on his mind, and that something was Lucinda. What do you think?"

"I think all this qualifies you as the world's champion standing-start-conclusion jumper of all time," she answered in a dispirited voice.

Tiredness was closing in on her like a fog. There was something she knew she ought to remember, something that nibbled at the edge of her exhaustion, but for the moment, she could not bring it out into the open.

"You look absolutely run into the ground," Dan said, "Don't you want to lie down for a while?"

"No, I want to keep talking. It's the only hope we have."

"Then how about a drink?"

"It might help at that. Vodka, please."

He poured the vodka and tonic and added ice. As he was handing her the drink, she suddenly knocked his hand aside and shot straight out of the chair. "Oh—oh—oh," she cried. "What a fool I am. What an idiot. That's the man!"

"Hey, that's pretty good vodka, and I never did like drinking it off the floor," Dan said mildly. "Now what man are you talking about?"

"Parker. He must have been the man on the lake."

"Who is Parker?"

"A guard at the prison. He's the one that I told you has gone out of his way to do all sorts of small things for Russ. He fits the description perfectly—stocky and fair-haired—and I'm sure he smokes cigars. He looks the type."

"Now I know you'd better go and lie down. You're really getting punchy, darling."

"But it's true. Parker must have been the man at the lake."

"To quote your own words, 'there are 38,000 stocky, fair-haired, cigar-smoking men in Okeechobee County.'"

"But not all of them knew Lucinda."

"And what makes you think this Parker did?"

"Because he was at her funeral. I saw him there. That was what I was trying to remember when I came home this afternoon, but until you began talking about the man in the boat, I was just too groggy to put it together."

"And do you mean to say that if this man had murdered Lucinda, he would then calmly proceed to attend her funeral?"

"Why not? Criminals have often shown more bravado than that in returning to the scene of the crime. Anyway, there is one more thing I can get checked out right now."

"What's that?"

"I can call the administration office at the prison and find out if Parker was on duty that day. If he was, then he was obviously not at the lake."

"And if he was not on duty?"

"It's still only a straw, but I'll clutch at anything now. Anything at all to save that boy."

The phone was in the hall. While she was using it, Dan fixed himself another drink. She was on the phone a long time, and he was halfway through his drink before she returned.

As soon as she entered the room, he could see the change in her. She was almost vibrating with excitement. "Do you know what they told me? On the twelfth—the day she was killed—Parker was not on duty. He had the day off. He told them in the office he was going down to the lake to go fishing"

"How do they happen to remember all that?"

"Because the twelfth was Parker's birthday, and they had all chipped in to buy him a box of cigars."

CHAPTER EIGHT

The eleven criminology students from the state university entered the death chamber through a back door. This was the usual procedure on guided tours of the prison since the warden felt, properly enough, that it would not be seemly to have these young people come face to face with men awaiting execution. They could look at the chair, but not at the men who would occupy it.

The room in which the executions took place was perhaps thirty feet square. It had only one small window set high on the east wall. The room was painted battleship gray and was scrupulously clean. At one end of the room were the chairs for the witnesses. At the other end, dominating the room like some medieval throne, stood the chair.

It has been said that anything that is truly functional has beauty. This may be true of a ball, of an ax handle, of a spoon; it is not true of the electric chair. Even without its frightful associations, it would still be ugly. It is rigid, massive, hung with straps. It is a giant's chair, far too big for any ordinary man. It could never be mistaken for anything but what it is—an instrument of torture.

Behind it, two handles project from the wall. These handles are perhaps twelve inches long and are painted a lighter gray. They control the charge that passes through the chair to the body of the man. Between the handles are four dials that register voltage and amperage.

Whenever his duties allow him to, the warden personally conducts these guided tours for students.

He considers it good policy, and also he rather enjoys it. He is a big, heavyset man with a head of wavy gray hair like that of a middle-aged matinee idol. And he always feels something like an actor, a little self-important, when he addresses his hushed audience in this big, square room.

"After the man's head has been shaved, his pant legs are slit, and then the electrodes are attached. This handle, here, controls the first charge and this one, here, gives him the second. The second charge is administered a few seconds after the first, and when it enters the body, the body jumps and twists, but the man does not really feel it. He hasn't felt anything at all after the first charge. The first charge has instantly paralyzed all his nerve ends. His heart may still be beating, and his body may still be moving, but the man is as good as dead. After that first charge, he feels nothing."

"May I ask a question, sir?"

"Why sure, son. What is it?"

"How do you know he feels nothing?"

"Well, of course, we have to go by what the doctors tell us."

"How many doctors who have been electrocuted have filed reports afterward describing their sensations?"

The warden gives the youngster a long, sharp look. There an uneasy silence in the still, cold room. The warden is not angry; he has been up against this sort of thing before. There is usually one in every crowd, and their bravado is easily deflated by the warden's massive dignity.

"The doctors have their way of estimating these things," the gray-haired man replies with deep-throated patience.

The boy, who has already decided to switch courses

next semester, anyway, does not go on with it. His courage trickles from him in this ghastly room. He has made a display of himself, and the others are staring at him curiously. He swallows audibly, the Adam's apple bobbing in his thin throat.

The professional photographer who has come with the group to take their picture and who is a short, fat man with a red, vulture-like beak, says in a loud voice, "How about a shot of the whole group around the chair?"

They gather together, grinning nervously. One of the boys who is a little braver than the others slips down into the cold, wooden embrace of the chair,

"Let's have a big smile."

The smiles are forced. Eleven bright-faced lads and lassies of the class of '63. There is a long silence in the room and then the burst of light from the flash bulb and the click of the camera shutter.

The outside door is opened and the students file wordlessly out. After the semi-gloom of the execution chamber, the sunlight is blinding. But once outside, their nervousness evaporates, and they begin to chatter among themselves.

The warden shakes hands with each of them in turn and then excuses himself. Unfortunately he cannot make the rest of the tour with them since he has other duties to attend to. However, Mr. Parker will be happy to answer any further questions.

The boy who asked the question about the doctors would like to ask one more but then thinks better of it. He has noticed how cold it was in the death chamber. He knows there is no air conditioning in the prison, and he would like to find out what gives that room its ghastly chill.

CHAPTER NINE

1

"I want to buy a shotgun, Pritchard," Dan said.

"We got us a nice selection, Mr. Waxman," the storekeeper replied. "This here Winchester is a right nice gun, but if you want somethin' less expensive, I could give you a Mossberg. Are you aimin' to use it on birds or rabbits?"

"Skunks."

"Well now," Pritchard said, blank-faced, "I wouldn't know 'bout that. Ain't many skunks 'round here that I know of."

"There have been quite a few around my place lately," Dan said. "I aim to run them off. I'll take the Mossberg."

"You want the shells too?"

"One box should do the trick."

Reaching for the box of shells Pritchard said, "And how is Miz Waxman these days?"

"Just fine."

"She still tryin' to get that boy off that killed his wife?"

"That's right," Dan answered brightly.

"Kinda runnin' out of time, ain't she?"

"Oh I don't know. She's uncovered some pretty interesting facts."

"That so?"

"How's the kerosene business these days, Pritchard?"

"Well, we don't sell much of it this time of year. Sell more of it come the cold weather."

"I had the idea people around here were using a lot

of kerosene lately."

"Not specially. But then, you never can tell. Kerosene business is liable to pick up any day now."

"Interesting," Dan said hefting the gun.

"Don't you want me to wrap that for you?"

"Why?"

"Folks might think it kinda strange to see you walkin' down the street with a shotgun."

Dan shook his head. "It's a nice gun. Nice and shiny. I want to show it off. See much of Lou Tayler these days?"

"Lou? Why no, no more'n usual."

"Well if you see him, you might mention the fact that I'm going skunk hunting."

Pritchard permitted himself a thin half-smile, the first Dan had ever seen him wear. "I guess Lou will be right interested to hear that."

"I bet he will," Dan said.

2

Circuit Judge Patrick J. Grady was on his way north to see the governor. He had not visited the governor in more than a year now, and what with his Perky case and one thing and another, he had decided that despite the fact that the governor's term was drawing to a close, it might still be a good idea to drop by to see him, and to mend a few political fences along the way.

It was late afternoon and he had been wheeling the big black air-conditioned Buick hard for a couple of hours along 27. At Haines City, feeling the first rumblings of hunger in his vast belly, he decided to swing west to Tampa for an early dinner at his favorite restaurant, *La Cubanita*.

Although he was still several miles away from the

eating place, his imagination was already hard at work on the *paella* he would order. Grady had two great weaknesses—food and women. And in both cases, his taste ran to the exotic, the highly spiced, the faintly dangerous. Tampa often satisfied both these cravings at the same time. After a tremendous meal at *La Cubanita*, he would pay a visit to his favorite whorehouse in Ybor City. Since he felt especially full of the juices of life today, he decided to make a complete evening of it, even if it meant an uncomfortably early start tomorrow, in order to be on time for his appointment with the governor.

The restaurant was spacious and cool and, like most Cuban eating places in Florida, painted pea green. On the walls were faded oil portraits of unknown Latin American military figures posing sternly under the awesome weight of epaulets and medals. Grady regarded the portraits of these military peacocks (the great majority of whom had never fought any kind of a battle) with a tolerant eye; he had a sneaking hunch that he resembled them in gravity and demeanor. Actually, nothing could have been further from the truth. Grady's judicial dignity was only a thin shell, to be stripped away at the slightest pretext. Given a pretty girl, a couple of drinks, a meeting of cronies, and he would revert at once to type—the roaring, backwoods bull—the wild black Irishman.

Amid a great deal of conversation with the owners and a good deal of bottom pinching with the waitresses, he packed away an enormous peppery meal and fortified it with half a bottle of bourbon. After dinner, he squeezed his bulk under the steering wheel of the Buick and steamed off to his favorite cat house.

The name of the place was *Azul Cielo* and it was

inhabited by as motley a crowd of fallen angels as a man might discover in a long night's looking. Mamacita, who ran the place, was almost as tall and as broad as Grady. But whereas the judge's flesh hung from his bones in pink folds, the madam was packed into her skin as tightly and sleekly as a new, brown sausage. She radiated health, love and avarice, and she had been dealing with men like Grady all her life, and knew them right to the depths of their strangest perversions.

The first room of the *Azul Cielo* was a public bar and the uninitiated, who did not know what was going on in the back rooms and the upstairs cubicles, might sit there and drink all night without being aware of just what errands of mercy these exceptionally friendly girls kept attending to. Behind the bar stood a huge, old-fashioned cash register, and behind the register, enthroned on a three-legged stool, sat the formidable Mamacita.

During the first few years in which he had been a patron of the *Azul Cielo*, Grady had made a fetish of anonymity. Obviously, although it was not unheard of, it would not do for a judge to be caught in a whorehouse. But as the years had gone by, and the police had been paid off regularly, his former fear of the place had been replaced by a sense of security and good fellowship. It was, therefore, no surprise to him when he heard Mamacita give a great shriek, "Gradee!" and saw her abandon her stool to come rushing toward him.

She threw her round, dark, naked arms around his neck and hugged his head between her immense breasts. The judge was aware of laughter throughout the room and of the musky odor of sweat mixed with cheap perfume. The heady fumes of bourbon and lust coursed through his slowly hardening arteries. He gave Mamacita a slap on her silk-clad bottom, and threw back his leonine head, and crowed like a rooster, while scraping the ground with his feet. This display was greeted with applause and drunken laughter from the crowd and shouts of "*Olé!*"

Proud as any bullfighter who has been awarded both ears and the tail, the judge strutted to the bar and downed a double shot of bourbon in two swallows. Sweat burst forth on his brow as if he had suffered an internal explosion.

"Much *hombre*, eh Mamacita?" he roared.

"Where 'ave you been, Gradee? We don' see you ver' long time."

"Aye, Mamacita. I am a big man. Important man. Do you think I can spend all my time in your lousy cathouse?"

"Hush, Gradee. Not so loud. Many people think is only nice bar here."

"Any fool thinks that, wouldn't know his ass from his elbow," responded the judge.

"Gradee. Gradee. You are terrible man. What is the matter with you tonight? You mus' be ver' dronk."

"A   dronk. Not so damned dronk as all that," the judge replied, imitating her accent.

"I theenk we do not see you because you 'ave another girl. You 'ave girl, Gradee?"

"Sure, I had a girl. I had the best-lookin' damned girl you ever saw."

"Then why you come 'ere? Where is thees bes'-lookin' damned girl? Maybe she 'ave another fellow, eh Gradee?"

"Not this one, Mamacita. This one is dead."

"You mean eet? She die?"

Grady nodded solemnly. For a moment, a mournful

look passed over his immense red face.

"What she die of? Maybe she die from too much Gradee, eh? Too much push-push, Gradee?"

"Her husband killed her, damn him."

"Er 'usband? Why he keel 'er? Why 'e no keel you, Gradee?"

"I guess he might have if he'd known about it," the judge replied.

The gaiety was leaving him, slowly being replaced by a vague sense of discomfort from the tremendous quantities of *paella* he had stuffed into his belly. With a sure instinct for keeping her customers happy, Mamacita decided to step up the pace.

"Come along, Gradee. We 'ave new picture for you. Ver' hot stuff. Wow! Also we 'ave new table. You love eet."

"Table? What kind of table?"

"You see. You see," Mamacita replied, herding him toward the passageway that led to the rear. "First you like to see the picture?"

"Why sure, honey. I ain't been to the movies in a coon's age."

He followed her great swinging buttocks up the narrow stairway to the projection room where a 16 mm movie projector had been set up on the racked enamel of an old kitchen table. In front of the projector was a double bed. On one wall was the screen; the other wall was occupied by a large mirror.

"Who you want to watch the movie with you, Gradee?"

"Why you, honey."

"No, no, Gradee. I am too much woman for you. We are friend, not the lover. I send you Rosita."

I would just as soon settle for a Bromo Seltzer, the judge thought unhappily. However, he did not voice the thought since it would surely mean a serious loss of face. "Great," he said. "And a little more of that rotgut bourbon of yours, Mamacita."

"Is no rotgut. Is good stuff, Gradee."

"Well whatever it is, send it on up with Rosita."

The hot, smoky room swam around him. Torrents of sweat oozed from his flesh. He felt undeniably ill now, but he was determined not to surrender to it. The bourbon was like gall in his mouth. He was only dimly aware of tiny, dark-haired, angelic-faced Rosita cuddling next to him and of the bored-looking, cigar-smoking projectionist standing behind the machine.

The cracked film progressed in jerky, badly lit sequences. On the screen, a large blonde was sprawled on an unmade bed. Enter a wiry little man nude, except for a Derby hat and socks. He enjoys a truly astounding genital development. "Superman," Rosita murmurs happily.

Superman removes his Derby, but prudently keeps his socks on. He and the blonde fly into each other's arms. He makes love to her. She makes love to him. They perform astounding feats from impossible positions. They are not so much lovers as gymnasts. The eye of the camera scurries after them like some frantic insect. The judge belches heavily. Rosita has her warm little hand inside his clothing, but he fails to respond. Why did he eat that damned *paella?* He knows from experience that it is far too spicy for him. Despite his Gargantuan appetite, he really has a delicate stomach. What is he doing here anyway, in this miserable whore's den?

The cracked film splits apart and the screen is struck blind. "*Momento*," murmurs the projectionist. The film resumes, but now it is running backwards. The lovers jerk away from each other and scuttle backward in crab-like nudity. Superman in the wrinkled socks retreats to his Derby hat and claps it onto his brow. The blonde lies once again in cavernous passivity. The projectionist mutters oaths and apologies. Grady roars with laughter. For the first time, he is really enjoying himself. Rosita giggles tentatively, and then she, too, is screaming with glee.

The projectionist grinds his cigar and vows, "I fix. I fix."

"Don't fix," bellows Grady. "It's better this way."

Mamacita has heard the row and comes pounding up the steps. She takes in the situation at a glance, and with the initiative the born showman, says, "You like, Gradee? You like?"

"Oh, by God, Mamacita. By God. That little bastard runnin' backward with that goddamned Derby hat. Oh, oh—" He cannot go on.

"Is ver' fonnee?"

"Funny? Funny? Oh my God!"

"You want to see table now?"

"Sure. Sure. Anythin'."

She leads the way down the stairs and into another back room where a bright, new, stainless steel obstetrical table has been set up. Mamacita is proud as punch of this new toy.

"Now what the hell is that?" Grady says in puzzled tones.

"You don't know, Gradee?"

"Hell no."

"Is for to make the examination. Rosita, show the judge."

Rosita, nimble as a faun, hops up onto the table and sticks her legs into the stirrups. The dress falls away from her naked thighs.

"I see," says Grady.

"Sure you see, Gradee. Everybody see. This way you don't buy, how you say, pig in a sack?"

"In a poke."

"Poke. Sack. What the hell."

"By God, it's a wonder, Mamacita. Now where is that goddamned bourbon?"

"Right here, Gradee."

"Now let's see the rest of them."

"Sure. Sure."

The whores are only too anxious to perform. One after the other they demonstrate their wares in the grip of the steel monster. Shrieks of laughter shake the walls.

"Now you, Gradee."

"Who? Me?"

"Sure. Sure. You are superman, no?"

Led by the indomitable Mamacita, they converged on the fat judge. A dozen pair of knowing hands clutch at him. In a twinkling his clothing is gone and he is maneuvered, howling and protesting, onto the table. His legs are thrust into the stirrups. His quivering, pink bulk is as flabby as that of a dead cow on a butcher's table. Mamacita pours the bourbon onto his open craw. He tries to shield himself with his hands but they are pulled away.

Mamacita stares at the blubbery mess with sudden blinding hatred and says, "Superman! Some superman!" All the withering contempt that lies behind years of catering to nameless obscenities is summed up in these words

"Cojones su me madre! Look at him. The biggest whore of all!"

3

Mamacita was panic-stricken. It was clear to her that Grady was dying. He lay twitching and groaning on the stainless-steel table. His vast face was suffused with blood; his flabby arms hung limp. They had played too rough with him, she had tried to tell them that, but the whores had gone a little crazy with this defenseless hulk at their mercy. It was as if all the years of hatred for men and what men had done to them was now to be vented on the judge. They had tickled him, pounced on him, roughed him up, kissed him, mouthed him and handled him while he had begged hysterically for a breather until suddenly his face had contorted in a spasm and he had let out a great moan and gone rigid.

Mamacita had driven the howling pack away from him but by that time it was too late. The years of overeating and sexual overindulgence had done their work on his heart. His eyes had rolled into the back of his head and one corner of his mouth was twisted in an ugly droop. He was having a stroke.

Now, as the madam stared down at him, she felt no pity for the judge, only for herself. How could she dispose of this three hundred pounds of blubber that was about to destroy her livelihood? If it had been anybody else, the police might have been bribed, but when a circuit judge died in a whorehouse, you could not hush it up.

The naked girls had stopped their giggling and prancing and stood in a semicircle staring down at the sick man.

"He don't look good," somebody said. "We better get the doctor."

Mamacita turned on her in a fury. "Doctor! No doctor! What you theenk, is leetle case of clap or something? Eef thees peeg die here they shut us up forever, an' all of you go back to peddle your ass on sidewalk."

"Maybe we take heem to hospital?" one of the other girls offered.

"No hospital! They ask too many question. Where he get seek? How? Who weeth heem? What they doin' to heem? Ees only one theeng. We got to get rid of heem. Get his clothes on heem. Get heem all dress. Queek! Rosita, get me José an Pepe."

Rosita pulled on the cotton dress over her head and scurried into the bar. She whispered to the two bartenders and they immediately followed her into the back room. There Mamacita explained in a few well-chosen words what she wanted done. Considering the gravity of the situation, she was remarkably succinct. If she had not been a woman and a whore, she might have made an admirable general.

Pepe's eyes grew round. "Jus' leave heem? What eef he is dead?"

"Alive or dead. Do as I say. Take heem in hees car out of town. Some place where nobody see you. Maybe the beach. Yes, the beach. Touch nothing. Take nothing from heem or I cut your heart out. Put heem behind the wheel of the car an leave heem there. You understan'? Good. Queek then!"

Pepe and José each got one of the judge's huge arms around their necks and hustled him out the back way. The car keys were in Grady's pants pocket. Jose's fingers lingered lovingly for a moment on the judge's wallet, but he remembered Mamacita's stern warning. Pepe held the judge propped against the wall while Jose backed the Buick into the alley. They put the judge into the front seat beside the driver. He slumped sideways and his head lolled back as if he were asleep. He was making a frightful snoring noise.

"You drive," Pepe said. "I follow."

José drove off at once while Pepe followed in Mamacita's canary yellow Cadillac convertible. They drove quickly toward the outskirts of town until they came to the beach road. There José turned west and followed the road down to the shore of the Gulf. Fortunately, at that hour the beach was deserted. They stopped the cars and Pepe helped José shift the judge into position behind the wheel. Then they turned and ran back to the convertible and drove quickly but discretely away by another road.

The judge was strangling in his own juice. Saliva flooded his mouth, but his rigid throat muscles made it impossible for him to dispose of it. Yet he was still horribly aware of what was happening to him. Despite the fact that he could not move, and could hardly breathe, he knew that the whores had abandoned him here to die.

The slow roll of the surf came to him as from a great distance. A car went by with a rush, and for a moment hope flared in his tortured breast as he thought it might stop, but then the sound was gone and he was alone again with the sea.

He tried to reach a hand out to the horn button, and by a monumental effort of will actually managed to push his fingers for an inch along his linen-clad knee, but beyond that he could not go. A great shudder racked his frame. The sea of juice welled up out of his throat. The eyes burst from his brick red face.

In another moment he was no longer aware of the sea or the passing cars or even of the whores' treachery.

4

Governor Harwood felt a distinct sense of relief when Judge Grady failed to show up for his appointment. It was always a chore, being with Grady. His immense vitality was overwhelming, and those small piggish eyes concealed a cruel and vengeful intelligence. The political woods were full of Gradys, and as a matter of survival, the governor had long since learned to deal with them; but still, particularly in the case of the judge, it went against the grain.

At what point, he wondered, did a man rise above this sort of thing, free himself of these political vultures? The answer, of course, was never. Right on up to the White House, he felt sure, it must be the same—a never ending procession of men to whom you owed favors—men who could swing votes—men who were important cogs in the party machine. People really imagined that when they elected a governor, they were electing one man to an important office. What they didn't know was that they were electing a thousand-and-one Gradys at the same time, and that it was these Gradys who made the governor, and that without them, he would vanish into political limbo.

Governor Harwood was a slender, good-looking man with close-cropped silver hair. Although his fifty-second birthday was only weeks away, he still weighed only three pounds more than he had as an undergraduate at Gainesville. And along with his uncommonly youthful appearance went a crop of modern ideas that were distinctly atypical of Southern governors. He had recently made something of a name for himself nationally as one of the more liberal of the new breed of Southerners. A speech in which he had, if not openly supported, at least not condemned the Negro lunch counter strikes, had made him the white-haired boy of the northern liberals. There was already some rather serious talk about running him in the second spot on the national ticket. And since, by law, he could not succeed himself as governor, he was understandably eager to enhance this national position. On the other hand, he had been in politics long enough to know that without the support of his own people, he would be dead. Party stalwarts like Grady and Dicky Miller, the State's Attorney, could still do him a great deal of harm if they were so minded. It would be better to stay on the right side of them.

Dicky himself was not politically powerful, but his father-in-law, old Robineau, certainly was. Robineau, ignorant cracker bastard that he was, owned half the grove land in the state. And it was Robineau money that had taken Dicky Miller to the state's attorney's office and might someday take him to the governor's mansion.

Dicky was a half-wit with a football player's shoulders and the big handshake, but whether you liked him or not wasn't the point—the point was he had the power. And, for that matter, so did Grady. Circuit judges are not ordinarily great political shakes, but Grady was the exception. He was very firmly entrenched down there in Okeechobee County, and it looked as though his patronage was responsible for half the state jobs in the area. Also he had managed to convey the impression that he knew where at least half the political skeletons in the state were buried. It was said that he had been present at some pretty wild parties and had kept a careful list of those who had attended. The governor had no personal knowledge on this score, but he was inclined to think that such a list did exist. Grady was certainly a lecherous old goat, and when he came to the state capital he usually checked into an obscure motel on the outskirts of town and kept a steady procession of tarts coming and going.

The governor pushed back his desk chair and rubbed the back of his neck. He felt tired and a little headachy. He wondered if he were coming down with one of those damned viruses that were all over town. He had to see so many people in his work and you never knew what sort of bugs they were toting around with them. Well there was one thing to be grateful for anyway, Grady had now missed his appointment altogether. Maybe, he thought with thinly disguised eagerness, something has happened to the old bastard.

CHAPTER TEN

1

"Miz Waxman?" the voice over the phone said.

"Yes, this is Mrs. Waxman."

"This is Aunt Bessie Carter, up to the lake."

"Oh yes, my husband told me about you. I want to thank you for trying to help us."

"Miz Waxman, I was wrappin' me some fish in the newspaper this morning an I seen somethin'."

Marty waited for her to go on, but there was only silence.

"What did you see Aunt Bessie?"

The phone made a series of odd digestive noises.

"Hello. Hello. Aunt Bessie?"

"I'm here, Miz Waxman."

"I was afraid you had hung up."

"No'm. I'm here."

"What was it you saw?"

"I seen a picture."

"What picture?"

"We havin' us real nice weather now."

"Yes, yes, I know. What picture?"

"Could be the man I saw in Mr. Perky's boat that day. Look a lot like him."

Her heart seemed to leap into her throat and hang there. After a long moment she was able to speak again. "What's his name?"

"Don' know."

"Well doesn't it say under the picture?"

"Maybe it do."

"Then for God's sake read it to me."

Aunt Bessie's chuckle was melodious and full-throated. "Can't do that, Miz Waxman."

"Why not?"

"Can't read."

"Oh." She felt a fool. Somehow she was always out of step with these people. "Well look, where are you calling from?"

"Garage."

"The garage at Pelican Bay?"

"Yes'm."

"Well there must be someone there who can read. What about the man who runs the place. You ask him to read the part under the picture for you."

"Sho'."

The silence seemed endless. Finally Aunt Bessie came back on and said, "You there?"

"Yes. I'm here. Did he read it for you?"

"He say the man's name is Farr."

"Mack Farr?"

"Yes'm."

"What does it say about him?"

"Say he killed a policeman."

"And you're sure he's the man you saw?"

"No'm."

"But isn't that what you just said."

"No'm. I say he look like him."

"I'm coming over to talk to you, Aunt Bessie. Will you stay where you are?"

"Yes'm."

"It will take me the better part of an hour. Will you wait?"

"Got no place to go," Aunt Bessie said.

Marty hung up. Her mind was whirling. Why Farr? Well why not Farr? From what Dan had told her, the old woman was no fool. But from a picture glimpsed while wrapping fish in a newspaper—good Lord were these the things on which a man's life hung …?

She dialed the state's attorney's office and asked for Mr. Miller.

"Who is calling please?" came back the coldly supercilious voice of bureaucracy.

"Mrs. Waxman."

"I'll see if he's in."

After a long pause she heard Miller come on and say, "Look, Mrs. Waxman, I don't want to be rude, but I've told you ten times there just isn't another darn thing this office can or will do about Perky. First the state was satisfied that he killed his wife, and then the jury was satisfied, and after that the court of appeals was satisfied. Now the governor has been satisfied too."

"Does that mean you've heard something?"

"The date of execution was established this morning."

"When is it?"

"The twenty-sixth. Ten o'clock in the morning."

"But that's only three days off."

"That's right."

"They can hardly wait to finish him off, can they?"

"I'd say that's pretty reckless talk, Mrs. Waxman."

"What would you say if I told you that Judge Patrick Grady knew the late Mrs. Perky very well? Maybe too well. Would you say that would be grounds for a mistrial?"

"It would, if you could prove it. Can you prove it?"

"Not yet. But I will."

"Then in the meantime, it's just hearsay. You're a lawyer; I don't have to tell you what that's worth. Now I have some people waiting in my office. Was that all you called to tell me, Mrs. Waxman?"

"One thing more, Mr. Miller," she said holding her temper firmly in check. "Can you tell me the date of Mack Farr's arrest?"

"What's he got to do with this?"

"Nothing. I just want to know when he was arrested."

"All right. My file is right here. Farr killed a police officer in Pahokee while attempting the holdup of a filling station. He was apprehended in the act. I certainly hope you're not trying to tell me he's innocent too."

"I'm not trying to tell you anything, Mr. Miller. I'm just asking for some information. When did the killing take place?"

"October 14th."

"Two days after Lucinda Perky was murdered."

"If you'll just tell me what you're after...."

"Nothing, Mr. Williams. Nothing at all. Thank you very much."

The receiver had barely settled into place before she was halfway out the door. She saw Dan and Meg walking slowly toward her along the road. Marty gunned the car down to them in second and slammed it to a stop.

"The Stirling Moss of Okeechobee county," Dan said. "I may enter you at Sebring next year. How do you do from a Le Mans start?"

"Something's come up. That woman you spoke to, Aunt Bessie, called me. She says she has a picture of a man who could be the one she saw in the boat that day."

"Who is it?"

"Farr."

"The cop killer?"

"Yes."

"Well I'll be damned. Do the dates check? I mean was he on the loose that day?"

"It looks that way. Anyway, I'm rushing over to talk to her. Can you handle Meg?"

"Sure."

"I probably won't be coming straight back. Anyway, I'll call."

"Good luck. And listen, keep it under eighty, will you?"

Marty roared off without an answer.

She found the garage at Pelican Bay without any trouble. It was a mile past the camp on the dead-end road that ended at the shore of the lake. The place was a shabby little Shell station flanked on either side by rusting wrecks and mounds of old tires that looked like some sort of primitive altars. The huge colored woman sat waiting patiently on an upended soft drink box in approximately a square foot of shade.

"Aunt Bessie?"

"That's me."

"Do you have the picture?"

A flicker of something that was half akin to sorrow passed across the great black face. "Yes'm."

Marty clutched at the wrinkled paper that was covered with dried fish scales. Despite the muck, the picture of Farr was clear enough. He stood, grinning arrogantly, between two deputies. It was the same half-contemptuous smile he had worn in prison the day he had crushed her hand. "You're reasonably certain this is the man, Aunt Bessie?"

"Could be him."

"Pictures can be deceptive. Do you think you would know him better if you saw him face to face?"

"How we gonna do that? He in jail, ain't he?"

"We might work it."

"Don't see how, 'less I goes to the jail. One thing sure, he can't come to me."

"Well that was what I had in mind—for you to go up to the state prison at Raiford."

"Ole judge ain't gonna like that."

"Ole judge doesn't have to know anything about it. Look, Aunt Bessie, you've got to quit worrying about that infernal Judge Grady. If you know something, and an innocent man's life is at stake, it's your duty to speak out. You have your rights, just as I do."

"You don't really believe that, do you?" Aunt Bessie said.

"About speaking out? Certainly."

"What you said about rights."

"Perhaps not. We can't fight that whole battle now. But we can fight one little part of it as one human being to another."

Aunt Bessie sighed, and in that sigh were all the unspoken years of misery and resignation. "It sho' is a mistake I'm makin'," she said. "I'll come, but I don't promise nothin' after that."

"I'm not asking you for any promises. I just want you to look at the man."

"Will we see Mistah Russ too?"

"Yes."

"All right. I'll come."

Marty opened the door for her, and with a kind of ponderous grace Aunt Bessie slid her vast, rippling body onto the seat.

2

When Aunt Bessie first saw the grim-looking prison walls topped by barbed wire and gun turrets, she said, "I sure don' like this place."

"Nobody likes it, but we're here to try to help Mr. Russ, and that's what we've got to bear in mind," Marty said. "Now here's what we're going to do. We're going to go inside to visit Mr. Russ, but while we're talking to him I want you to take a good look at the man in the cell next to him."

"Is that the man in the picture?"

"Yes, that's Farr."

"All right, I'll look at him."

"But try not to let Farr know that's what you're there for. I mean just sort of glance over at him without making it too obvious. Don't let him think you're there for any reason except to visit Mr. Russ. Do you understand?"

"I do it all the time, Miz Waxman."

"You do? How?"

"Fishin. I got to show the fish the bait without lettin' him know I'm there."

"That's the idea."

They waited at the front gate until Parker, immaculate as ever in a freshly pressed uniform, came toward them. Marty stood a little to one side carefully watching Aunt Bessie. Had the wise old eyes, half-hidden by the bulging cheeks, widened at the first sight of the guard?

"Hello, Mrs. Waxman," Parker said.

"How are you today, Ben?"

"You picked a pretty hot day for a long drive."

"I'm afraid I don't have much choice anymore."

"Yeah, I just heard about it. It's Tuesday, isn't it?"

"Yes. Ben, this is Aunt Bessie Carter. She lives up near the camp and she's one of Russ's old friends. Will it be all right if she comes in with me for a minute?"

"Well, you know we have special rules concerning visitors to the death house; but I guess if she's with you it will be all right."

"Thank you, Ben. I appreciate it."

"It's little enough. I wish there were something else we could do."

"I guess you've helped him more than anyone. He told me about it. You've been a real friend to him. You know, I was wondering about that. Are you so attentive to all the prisoners?"

Parker shook his head.

"Then why Russ?" she asked.

"I guess mostly because he's just a kid. I'm a guard here, but that doesn't keep me from having feelings. I feel damned sorry for him."

"Don't you think he did it?"

"You know better than to ask me that."

"All right, so I know better. But I want to ask you anyway. What difference can it make now?"

"I'll say this much, I think he's getting a raw deal."

"Well that's something, isn't it? In what way is he getting a raw deal?"

"So far as I now, the evidence against him was purely

circumstantial. I figure on that basis he should have been given a recommendation of mercy."

"Why do you think he wasn't?"

"How would I know?"

"Do you think it could have been political influence?"

Parker shrugged his shoulders slightly and looked away, across the compound. "Could be."

"I'm not trying to back you into a corner, Ben. I realize how tricky your position necessarily must be." Ah, deceitful female, she thought. Mother of all whores. "But I did want you to know that I'm grateful to you for being kind to him in these last weeks. Does he ever talk about his place up at Pelican Bay?"

"Not too much."

"It's a very lovely spot. I think you're the kind of man who would appreciate it. Do you ever do any fishing, Ben?"

"Sure. I love fishing. I don't often get the chance, but when I do I grab it."

"Did you ever fish anywhere around Okeechobee?"

"I've been there."

Well that was noncommittal enough. She had the feeling that she might be pushing the thing a little too far, and rather than alarm him at this point, she decided to back away from it. They exchanged a few more words of no particular significance, and then Parker was ringing the button in the otherwise blank wall, and the face of the man in the turret was peering down at them through the sun-glazed glass.

When they had been passed through the two doors into the corridor that led to Russ's cell, all three of them inadvertently began to walk softly, respectful in the near presence of death. They found Russ lying on his side in the bunk with his back to them. In that position, reminiscent of the fetus, he looked painfully young and defenseless. The image of his body strapped into the chair and writhing under the impact of high voltage appeared in Marty's mind and brought tears to her eyes. For a moment she was afraid she would not be able to go through with it, but then Parker was saying, "Mrs. Waxman to see you, Russ."

Russ had not been asleep. He nodded his head, but before he turned toward them, she saw his hand creep up to his eyes. He, too, had been crying. When at last he turned toward them, his face was haggard, but he managed to pull himself together and smile at her. This was always the most difficult moment for her, when he seemed to feel it necessary to cheer her up. Then he saw the bulk of Aunt Bessie beside her and said with surprise, "Why it's Aunt Bessie."

"Sho' is, Mistuh Russ."

"How are you, Aunt Bessie?"

"Jus' fine. How you makin' out, Mistuh Russ?"

"I guess I'm all right."

"Fishin' mighty good at the lake now. Had us a little northeaster a couple days ago, and it seemed like it stirred them up. They bitin' good all over the lake. And your camp in good shape too, Mistuh Russ. Everythin' jus' fine over to your way."

Russ did not answer.

"Yessir, everythin' jus' fine," the Negro repeated vaguely, letting her eyes wander over toward the next cell where Farr was watching them from between the bars.

"I'm keepin' an eye on everythin' for you, Mistuh Russ," Aunt Bessie went on. "You be glad to see it when you comes back."

Russ's face crumpled and he turned away from them. Marty motioned to Aunt Bessie to start back down the corridor.

"It's all right, Russ," Marty said softly. "Something new has come up. It changes the whole complexion of the case. The governor will simply have to grant you a stay. He'll have no choice."

The words lacked conviction and Russ did not bother to answer. Instead he turned away and went back to the cot. She waited a moment and then followed Aunt Bessie out through the door.

When they left Parker at the gate Marty was aware that he was still watching them. She said nothing to Aunt Bessie until they were back in the car and then asked, "Well?"

"Can't say for sure," Aunt Bessie said, shaking her head. "Could be him. Look a lot like him. Course he was quite a far piece away from me that day in the boat."

"You've got to make up your mind. This way it's no use to us."

"One thing I is sure of."

"Well thank God for small favors. What is it?"

"That Mr. Parker. I knows I seen him befo'. Seen him to Miss Lucinda's funeral. Seen him many a time around Belle Glade befo' that."

3

Dan awoke to the sound of rain and the rumble of a car on the road. He got out of bed and went to the window but could see no lights. Yet the sound of the car, an old car if you could judge by the grinding of the transmission and the going in second along the dirt road that led down toward the concrete tomato troughs, persisted. Obviously, whoever was in the car was up to no good, prowling around that way with their lights off.

He tiptoed to the door of the other bedroom and peeked in at Meg. She was sleeping quietly with her arms around Baby, the old rag doll that she had cherished since infancy. He closed her door and then, on second thought, turned the key in the door and took it out of the lock and left it on the kitchen table.

He pulled on a pair of khaki pants and sneakers and his old raincoat, then picked up the shotgun that was standing in the corner. He got out the box of shells, broke the gun and leaded it. The remainder of the shells he dropped into the pocket of the raincoat. After that he took a long four-battery flashlight off its hook in the kitchen closet, tested it to see that it was working properly and then dropped it into the other pocket.

He felt a little foolish, a little theatrical. His heart was thudding with excitement and his hands were cold. Waxman the warrior. A lanky man with tousled hair and a big nose and wearing pajama tops and sneakers and a not-too-clean raincoat. The gun in his hand was heavy and oily and, in a way, more alarming than reassuring. He did not want to kill anybody. For that matter, he did not even want to hurt anybody; but he had put all their futures, his own and Marty's and Meg's, into these tomatoes and squash and cucumbers, and he would not lie shivering with trepidation in his bed while some miserable cracker son of a bitch destroyed them.

There was no question in his mind that that's what it was all about, this car coming in late at night with its lights off. They were after his crop. He had hoped that his well-advertised purchase of the shotgun would be enough to scare them off, but apparently it had failed.

He let himself out of the back door and stood

listening. He could no longer hear the sound of the motor. He stood there in the rain thinking, what the hell, why should I get involved in a shooting scrape for some lousy vegetables? Anyway, it's wrong of me to leave the house; I really ought to be here with Meg if she wakes up. Let them have the damned crop. At best it had been only a foolish dream, like Marty's dream of saving Russ. And now both dreams were going down the drain. Well let them go. To hell with it. They could pack their things and go back to New York where they belonged. Who needed all this? What did it prove anyway?

But of course he knew very well what it proved. It would prove once and for all that he was sans guts. The tired Jewish intellectual sitting on a park bench carping at the state of the world and baying at the moon.

Except that not all the Jewish intellectuals were sitting on park benches. On the shores of the sea of Galilee, at Nebeusha or Kvorshaba, there were other farmers who were out tonight protecting their crops with guns in their hands. Men like himself, probably, some of them nervous and ungainly and unwarriorlike, with worried minds and cold hands. They had lived, many of them, through things that were beyond the comprehension of the simple mind. Yet they had not broken, and they had not run away, and they were not taking anything lying down. They had picked up their guns the way farmers always had to pick up their guns when things got rough, and now they were out protecting their wells, their equipment, their crops, their homes and their land.

Was he less of a man than they? Was he ready to turn the other cheek and say, spit on me, kick me? It would be so easy to go back into the house now and huddle there while these thin-lipped bastards destroyed the growing creation of his mind and sweat. But even while he questioned himself, he knew it was too late for that now; there was no turning back.

Holding the oily gun very tightly, he stepped out into the rain, away from the house.

The troughs, there were three of them, were like huge concrete coffins, each one hundred feet long and six feet wide. They contained no soil for the growing of vegetables, but only a mixture of water and fertilizers. The plants were suspended above on a wire screen and sent their roots down toward the life-giving mixture. It was an artificial method and extremely costly, so far as the capital investment was concerned, but it had enormous possibilities. It was his conception of the future applications that always fascinated Dan. For if the method could be proven to be practical, and he had already demonstrated that he could produce tomatoes, cucumbers, squash and melons superior in size and quality to those grown by conventional methods, it would mean that men would no longer have to confine their farming to the comparatively few fertile areas of the world. Instead hydroponic bins could be erected on even the rockiest and most forbidding land, producing a bumper crop of fresh food to meet the world's ever-growing birthrate. This was the dream he had brought down with him from New York, and now that it was on the verge of reality, he was not ready to surrender it all at the first sign of force.

He could make out the car now, an even blacker shape against the darkness. From the dimly seen outline, high and boxy, he guessed it to be an old car, an old Buick or Hudson or Chevy.

Moving the gun over to his left arm he got out the

flash and shone the beam of light at the rear of the car. There was a license but it was smeared with mud. He moved closer, intending to wipe off the plate in order to read the numbers, when something big and black came swooping down at him like a great bird. He turned to face it, half-throwing up his right arm in a defensive gesture; but it was too late. The blow took him on the side of the head, spun him around and knocked him to his hands and knees in the mud.

His skull rang like a bell. Lights flickered before his eyes. He was vaguely aware of voices in the night and the rush of feet. He tried to stand, but his legs had no muscles. For the moment, there was no pain, just an inability to command his limbs.

Finally he lurched to his feet and picked up the shotgun and still had sense enough left to cock it. When he fired, the recoil knocked him over again. The blast was deafening.

The car was in gear now and swinging around. He shouted after it, but the sound of his voice was lost in the rain. He saw the square blackness of the car turn and head for the road. He aimed in the general direction of the car and let fly with the other barrel. This time, above the thunder of the gun, he distinctly heard the smash of glass.

But the car kept moving, and while he was still fumbling for the shells in his pocket, it had gone over the crest of the rise and was out onto the main road, tearing back toward town. He waited a long moment to see if they might come back, but he knew, happily, that he had routed them. He retrieved the flash from the muddy ground and groped forward after the long finger of yellow light.

It was quickly apparent that this had not been a simple kerosene-dumping expedition. At the base of the first trough, lying at an angle against the cement where they had dropped it in their haste, was a narrow cylindrical object, twelve inches long. At one end there was a fuse that gave it the appearance of a firecracker. Dynamite. One blast from this and the trough would have been blown to hell, and along with it, his entire project. He searched quickly, but carefully, around the other troughs to see if they had left any more explosives, but that first stick was the only one he found. Apparently he had run them off before they could prepare the others. He picked up the dynamite and carried it gingerly down to the reservoir pond below the troughs and tossed it out into the water.

Although his head was beginning to hurt abominably, he felt decidedly cheerful. He had defeated the barbarians. They knew now that he meant business, and it did not seem likely that they would be back for another taste of shot. He had not run from the challenge, nor had he squatted on his tail bemoaning his fate. He had given the bastards something to think about, and there was every reason to suppose the lesson had been driven home. At the same time, he had resolved many of his own doubts, tapping secret, inner reservoirs of strength.

Feeling only a little less than eight feet tall, and whistling merrily between his teeth, he strolled back through the rain to the house.

He unlocked the door to the little girl's room and found her still sleeping peacefully, completely undisturbed by the racket outside. He bent down and kissed her gently on the forehead, then crossed over to the bathroom and switched on the light above the basin and examined his head in the mirror.

Whatever they had clubbed him with had not done any great damage. There was a small abrasion of the skin in one area and a trickle of blood had mingled with the rain on his forehead. He washed the wound and dabbed it gingerly with a colorless antiseptic. When the stinging had eased off, he gulped a couple of aspirins to kill the headache and then went back to the kitchen to put on a pot of coffee.

He was finishing the last sip when he heard another car coming. He put down the cup and crossed to the window, but this time the car had its lights on. It was coming fast through the rain, too fast. He was expecting it to go on by, but to his surprise it slowed at the turn and swung in toward the house. Even before he saw the side of the car in the beam of light from the kitchen window, he recognized by the sound of the exhaust that it was Marty's station wagon.

When she was in the kitchen, looking wet and tired, her face drawn with strain, she said, "What are you doing up at this time of night? Is there something wrong? Is Meg ...?"

"Meg is fine. Sleeping peacefully. But where are you coming from in such a rush?"

"Tallahassee."

"Well why didn't you spend the night there?"

She wiped a hand across her brow and said, "I'll tell you in a minute. But first I could do with a cup of that."

"Coming right up."

"And I want to get out of these awful clothes."

Half-blind with fatigue, she stumbled across to the bedroom, peeked in at Meg and blew her a kiss, then stripped off her dress and stockings and put on a robe and slippers. When she was back in the kitchen, Dan said, "Now tell me, why are you racing around at one o'clock in the morning?"

"I just had to get home. I felt so tired and lonesome

and discouraged that the thought of spending another night alone in a motel room was enough to make me blow my top."

"What about Aunt Bessie? Did you take her to see Farr?"

"Yes. And she thinks she—" For the first time she became aware of Dan's appearance and of the soaked raincoat spread over the kitchen chair. "Well, what have you been up to? Taking a quiet little stroll in the cool night air?"

"Just checking."

"Checking what? You were never the type to go chasing shadows at one A.M."

Very briefly, omitting any mention of the dynamite, he told her what had happened.

"And you really fired that cannon?" she asked.

"That I did."

"Oh my. Do you suppose you winged them?"

"I feel reasonably sure that somewhere in this county there is an old jalopy minus a back window and with a shotgun-peppered stern.

"But your poor head."

"I don't even feel it."

"I think I'm kind of proud of you tonight, Mr. Waxman. Isn't it strange to be proud of your husband just because he pulls the trigger on a shotgun?"

"Never knew you were so bloodthirsty. Anyway, you know me and guns. I'm just glad I didn't shoot myself. Now what about you? I think you must be crazy driving down around the lake alone at this hour of the night."

"Oh, I'm all right."

"Sure you're all right. Until something happens."

"Like what?"

"Like anything. You're certainly not going to do Russ

Perky or yourself any good if you're lying cracked up in a ditch somewhere. That's a nasty stretch of road even on a dear night. I thought you had more sense."

"I know, and you're right, of course. But don't scold me, Dan. I just don't have the strength for it."

"All right, honey, I'll get off your back. But now tell me what's happened."

"Russ goes to the chair in just about fifty-six hours."

"Damn."

"I saw the governor this afternoon, but for all the good it did, I might as well have stayed home."

"Did you tell him about Farr?"

"I did better than that. I took Aunt Bessie up there with me to give him her side of the story. We got just exactly nowhere with him. His argument was that all we had to go on was supposition, and of course, from his standpoint he's quite right. We certainly have no concrete evidence to prove the identity of the man Aunt Bessie saw out on the lake that day. That is, if she saw such a man."

"Do you doubt it?"

"Not really, but what I doubt is our ability to uncover him in time to do any good."

"You look done in. Don't you want to go to bed now, and talk it over again in the morning?"

"There's no time for that," Marty said. "I want to talk it over now, so that by morning we'll know exactly what we have to do."

"How about a drink then? It might relax you."

"Brandy?"

"Wonderful."

He got out the bottle of Remy Martin and poured a jigger into her coffee and then one into his own. "Tell me about the governor," he said while he recapped the bottle. "What's he like?"

"Nice enough. Youngish. Very polite. Even goes so far as to say that he personally fails to see the value of capital punishment, and that the night before a man is to be executed, he, the governor that is, roams the streets all night trying to come to terms with his own conscience."

"A pretty speech."

"Well, I think he was sincere about it."

"Then why doesn't he do something?"

"What? His hands are tied. So long as the legislature refuses to do away with capital punishment, the governor obviously has to enforce the law."

"You make it sound very simple. Does that mean you've given up the idea that political forces have been at work in this case?"

"Not at all. I still see the fine hand of Grady all through this thing."

"So where do we go from here?"

"I don't know," she answered wearily. "If I can't get a stay of execution, I'm licked."

"Not by a long shot, you're not. Now tell it to me slow and easy, I mean about the governor and all that. Maybe I can make some sense out of it. Exactly what did he tell you?"

"As I told you, he gave me a long lecture on the evils of capital punishment. He even has all the details handy, like the fact that in England in the year 1800 there were more than 200 offenses punishable by hanging, including such relatively obscure crimes as poaching, cutting down somebody else's tree and associating with gypsies. In 1801, for example, a little boy named Andrew Benning who was not yet thirteen was hanged for entering a house and stealing a spoon.

"The governor was also full of information along the lines that today capital punishment has been abolished throughout most of western civilization. In western Europe it survives only in Britain, France, Ireland and Spain. While here in America, six states have done away with it altogether and a good many others are more or less on the fringe. He says that it is barbaric, savage, immoral, irreligious and a wasted effort since no one has ever been able to prove that it is a genuine deterrent to crime.

"But after it was all over, I gathered that the sum and substance his entire lecture was that he either cannot or will not do one single damned thing to save Russ Perky from the chair."

"He actually said that?" Dan asked.

"Not in so many words, but the message was certainly plain enough."

"Unless, of course, you can prove that there really was another man at the camp that day."

"I would be inclined to doubt it even then. From the way he sounded, I should think I would actually need a signed confession from the murderer."

"And that brings us back to Farr. What about him?"

"Aunt Bessie says it could be, but she won't swear to it. What she will swear to however is Parker."

"The guard?"

"Yes."

"You're kidding? You mean she will testify that Parker was at the camp that day?"

"Not at all. And even if she did, it wouldn't be enough to save Russ. No, what she means is that she saw Parker in the area at one time or another. And, of course, we both saw him at the funeral."

"Well, that's not much help, is it?"

"Not for the time we have left."

"Do they really look so much alike?"

"Parker and Farr? From a distance, yes. They have

the same general outline, fair-haired and sturdy. Close up, however, there's quite a difference. Farr is much tougher looking. What I mean is that Parker would seem to be perfectly capable of handling himself in a scrap, but in Farr there's a real hard core, a kind of steely quality that the other man lacks."

"But that doesn't mean that Parker might not be your man."

"Of course it doesn't. And if he were, it would explain his really extraordinary attitude toward Russ. He could hardly be treating him with any more consideration if he were his own son. Obviously he doesn't handle all the prisoners that way, so why Russ? There's got to be a reason."

"You mean he's considerate to the husband because he murdered the wife?"

"Is it so farfetched?"

"No more farfetched than any other theory we have to go on. But how do you get it out of him? Just take the bull by the horns and ask him straight out?"

"It might work."

"You mean you expect him to stick his neck into the noose, just like that?"

"Hardly. But there might be something in his reaction that would give me a clue."

Her eyes were half-closed. She had to blink them repeatedly to stay awake.

"I'll give you a clue right now," Dan said. "You're going to bed."

"Would it be beastly of me?"

"Frightful. But you certainly can't do Russ any good at three in the morning, and you will need some kind of a clear head tomorrow."

"I don't know why I'm so beat up. I feel as if somebody had taken out all my insides and tied knots in them. Will you hold me, Dan? Will you comfort me?"

"You will find me the most comforting guy in town."

"Tomorrow I'll have another go at the windmills. But not tonight. Tonight I am dead."

"Can you kick your shoes off?"

"Mmm."

"You're not helping any."

"What? Oh that. Don't you know how to undress a woman, darling?"

"I must be a little out of practice."

He bent down, put an arm under her, picked her up and carried her into the bedroom.

CHAPTER ELEVEN

1

"I didn't come to see Russ this time," Marty said. "What I really wanted was to talk to you."

"All right," Parker said. "What would you like to talk about?"

"Can we sit down somewhere?"

"How about down there by the recreation area?"

"That would be fine."

They walked across the blazing hot compound where a dozen or so prisoners lolled dispiritedly and sat down on one of the long benches that had been placed in the shade of the tin roof. The guard took a package of cigarettes out of the breast pocket of his shirt and offered one to Marty.

"Thanks," she said. "And thanks again for bringing those stamps to Russ."

"It was little enough."

"But more than you do for most of the others."

"I guess so."

"You knew Russ, didn't you?"

Parker removed his hat, wiped the leather band with his handkerchief and then replaced it on his head. "I was wondering when you'd get around to that," he said.

"Well didn't you?"

"No."

"You didn't know Russ before he came here?"

"No. I knew his wife."

The band music had begun again. Once more the sprightly strains of the *River Kwai* came floating across the compound. A team of prisoners lackadaisically pushed a roller over the ball field. To Marty, the whole thing seemed unreal, even Parker's confession that he had known Lucinda Perky had a dreamlike quality.

She waited for him to go on, but when he said nothing more, she asked sharply, "Well?"

"What is it you want to know?" the guard asked in a tired voice.

"Everything."

"I'm telling you now it won't save your client. I didn't kill Lucinda Perky."

"And if you had, you obviously wouldn't be admitting it. The day Lucinda was killed was your birthday and you had the day off. Where did you go that day?"

He turned to face her and asked in a voice that had in it more curiosity than unfriendliness, "Suppose I tell you to go fly a kite?"

"Then I go straight to the warden to tell him everything I know. After that, he can ask you the questions. Is that the way you want it?"

He shook his head. "No."

"Then you'd better start telling me how, when and

where you figure in the Perky case."

"I'll start at the end and work backwards. To begin with, I had nothing to do with her death. The day she was killed I was down on the north fork of the St. Lucie River fishing for snook. There were two other guards from the prison with me. They were with me from six o'clock in the morning when we left here until we got back at eight o'clock that night. During that time I wasn't out of their sight. We checked in at Burt Pruitt's fishing camp on the St. Lucie and rented a boat from him. His records will confirm that. Pruitt's place is about a hundred miles from where Lucinda was killed. My car was parked in plain sight in Pruitt's backyard the entire day. There was no way in the world I could have gotten from his place up to Pelican Bay. Does that answer your question?"

"If it checks."

"It will check."

"We'll see. Now I'd like to hear the rest of it. How did you know Lucinda?"

"The same way every other man knew her. But first let me explain something to you. Your threats about talking to the warden don't worry me. I'm sick of this job anyhow. I thought I had the stomach for it, but I don't. I'm quitting the end of the month. So don't think you've got me scared with all this talk of wardens and witnesses and so forth. I've known all along that you saw me at Lucinda's funeral, and that eventually you'd get around to putting two and two together. But that doesn't worry me."

Quite suddenly, she rather liked him. He was a stubby little man with hard, square hands and cold eyes, but there was something indestructibly honest about him. She knew instinctively that he was telling her the truth, and to her surprise she felt rather relieved.

"But what I am scared of and what does worry me is that my wife will find out what you already know."

"About Lucinda?"

"Yes."

"Want to tell me?"

"If you're satisfied with my story, and if the whole thing checks out, does it end here?"

She nodded.

"I'm thirty-nine years old," Parker said. "That's a bad age for a man. When you're pushing forty you begin to get all sorts of funny ideas about being over the hill. Maybe that was what started it. Or maybe it was just one of those things. I don't know. All I know is that I didn't go looking for it. Up to that time Marge and I were as happy together as we had any right to expect to be. But we had been married for twelve years. Maybe that had something to do with it.

"Anyway, it was several months ago that I saw Lucinda for the first time. It was my day off and I had gone over to the lake to do some fishing. I was driving back through town when I saw this girl coming out of the hardware store. She was wearing tight dungarees and a man's shirt knotted at the waist, with the two top buttons open. Did you ever see her?"

"Only once."

"Even if you only saw her once, it was enough to give you a pretty fair idea. Except for the girls you see in the movies—and I wonder what they would look like walking around town in old clothes—nobody around here, and that goes for me too, had ever seen anything like her. I can't tell you exactly what happened to me. I still don't know. After all, I'm no kid. But that one quick glimpse of Lucinda just knocked me for a loop. I felt as if I'd been clubbed with something. Almost without knowing why I was doing it, I turned the car around and began following her down the street. Even though she never turned around to look at me she knew I was there, and why. And I knew she knew.

"In the middle of the next block she turned into the entrance to the drugstore. I stopped the car and watched her through the store window. She sat at the counter and drank a coke. Then, for the first time, she raised her eyes and looked right out through the window at me. That one look was enough. All of a sudden I was like a sixteen-year-old kid, my heart pounding and my hands sweaty. I parked the car and went into the store and sat down on the stool next to her. In five minutes we were chatting like old friends about the weather and fishing and what a crummy town it was and everything like that.

"She was easy to talk to. I guess she was about the easiest woman to talk to I ever met. Later I realized it was because she'd had more experience talking to strange men than all the girls I'd known put together. Anyway, we had another coke and talked some more and she told me her name and that she was married. I asked her if we couldn't meet again and she said it might be arranged. But at some place safe. So I told her I'd be up there again next week, and she told me to meet her at a place called the Jockey Club about a mile out of town.

"That next week was a rough one. I was really sweating it out. I was like a kid on his first date. Just thinking about her would put me all on edge. I'd wake up in the night shaking with excitement. Marge and I have always had fewer quarrels than most married people, but that week I was like a sick dog, snapping and snarling. She could hardly open her mouth before

I'd jam the words back down her throat. She kept asking me what was wrong, but of course I couldn't tell her.

"Anyway, the great day finally came. I got to the Jockey Club and sat there for three hours. Lucinda never came. And I did something I hadn't done in years; I went on one beautiful binge. I got so drunk they had to look in my wallet to find out who I was, and after that they called Marge, and she came over on the bus to drive me home. Now what do you think you would do if you found your husband in that condition?"

"I'm not sure. Probably murder him."

"Well, I can tell you what Marge did. She never mentioned it. Not from that day to this. But, of course, I was too fouled up then to appreciate it. I had the feeling that she was being silent just to make me feel more guilty. And Lucinda was still under my skin. Despite the fact that I felt like a cheap heel, I still knew damn well that come my next day off, I'd be over there again trying to find her.

"I decided to give the Jockey Club one more try, and this time she was there. She was alone at the bar when I got there. She never said anything about that broken date, and I was too scared of antagonizing her to ask her. We sat around and had a few drinks, but she wouldn't let me touch her. The best I could get was an agreement to meet again the following week.

"Talk about kid stuff; there I was like some damned fool pup wagging its tail like an idiot for a pat on the head. A grown man. A family man. A guy who loves his wife and kids. How do you explain it?"

"I don't know," Marty said, "but you're certainly not the first to whom it has happened."

"I knew I had to have that girl if my life depended

on it. But I couldn't make her out. She was leading me on, and at the same time holding me off. In that kind of a game she held all the cards. And she played them just right. But the third time I saw her she sprang the big surprise. She said, 'Since you seem so set on it you can have me, but it will cost you.' Just like that, mind you. No beating around the bush. A damned cold-blooded whore. She even laid the price right on the line. A hundred dollars. For a hundred dollars she would meet me at a motel.

"Something died in me a little right there. I knew then it wasn't going to be the great love of my life and that I wasn't going to leave Marge and the kids for her. In that sense she did me a favor. But still I had to have her, no matter what the price. If she had asked a thousand, I would have mortgaged the car, or something, to raise the money.

"I asked her what she wanted the money for, and she shrugged her shoulders and said, 'What does anybody want it for? To get away. To get out of this lousy hole. But I've got to do it right. I don't want to wind up hustling drinks in some dive or busting my arches selling girdles in a department store. I want to check into the biggest, flashiest hotel in Miami and not give a damn what it costs. That way I'll make the right connections. There are an awful lot of rich old geezers down there who can keep me in the style to which I am not accustomed. But I need money to start the ball rolling. You can't get into that league without making a big splash. I'll need about five thousand bucks for clothes and everything until I get settled.'

"And is this the way you plan to get it?" I asked her.

"'Look,' she said, 'what have you got to be so goddamned righteous about? You're cheating on your wife, aren't you?'

"I think right then I might have killed her. But I didn't. I paid what she asked."

Marty waited for him to go on. Parker sat staring moodily at the sunburnt grass. Finally, Marty said, "And?"

"That was the only time. Just that once. I never saw her again. The closest I ever came to her after that was when she was in her coffin. It wasn't always easy. I had to fight like hell against the temptation to go back to her. That day she was killed, on my birthday, I almost started out to see her. But I had made up my mind not to have anything more to do with her and I stuck to it. Except for the funeral. She was a bitch, but she was beautiful and unhappy and I felt I owed her that. The same way I feel I owe Russ something. He didn't make her what she was, and I don't know if he killed her or not, but in my own way I took something away from him, and I have to do what I can to pay back a little part of it.

"If you don't believe me I'll have to prove what I said, I mean about not seeing her again after that one time. But the only way I can prove it is to bring in witnesses, and if I do that Marge will surely know about it, and that will be the end for us. I don't want that to happen. I don't want all the good years with Marge to go down the drain because of that damned whore Lucinda."

"Does that mean you're prepared to see Russ die for the same reason?"

"There is nothing I can do for Russ beyond the little things I try to do for him here. I didn't kill his wife and I don't know who did."

"Do you think there were other men who were involved with her the same way you were?" Marty asked.

Parker nodded slowly. "There must have been. She said she wanted to put together a stake of four or five thousand dollars, and there was only one way in the world a woman like Lucinda could get hold of that kind of money."

"Do you know who the men were?"

"We never discussed it."

"What do you know about Mack Farr?"

"Not much. Only what everybody else knows. He killed a cop."

"Do you know where he was or what he was doing before that?"

"He was in the army. I read where he was quite a war hero."

She shook her head and said, "I'll tell you something, I'm a rotten lawyer."

"In what way?"

"I'm inclined to believe the story you told me about yourself and Lucinda. If I was a better lawyer, I'd tear you to shreds on it."

"What I told you is the truth."

"I'd like to meet your wife some time. She must be quite a gal."

"She is."

"I've changed my mind. I'm going to blackmail you just a little bit after all. It's about Farr."

"What about him?"

"I'm not sure yet, but I think there's a possibility Farr may be mixed up in this thing too. I don't know how, but I mean to find out. When the time comes I will probably need your help."

"I'll be here," Parker said.

2

"Think, Aunt Bessie. There must be something. Some little thing you've overlooked."

"Done tole you everthin' I know, Miz Waxman."

"Have you still got that picture of Farr?"

"Yes'm."

"There is something about it that keeps nibbling away at the back of my mind. Can we have another look at it?"

"Sho'."

They were in Aunt Bessie's one-room shack. Although the outside had never known a coat of paint the inside was neat as a pin. On one wall was a small whitewashed fireplace. Above it, on the brick mantel, a small, round pink box bearing the label, "Lady Cashmere Face Powder". On the wall above that was a picture clipped from a calendar. It showed a little girl in a long white nightgown kneeling between her mother's knees with her hands clasped. The mother gazed fondly down at her. The title of the picture was "Just a Prayer at Twilight". The only furniture in the room, apart from a pot-bellied stove, was a rocker and a brass bed.

Marty's eyes took in these details but her mind was elsewhere. The picture of Farr. That confounded picture. She smoothed it carefully and held it to the light to study each detail. But there was nothing about it that was of help to her.

Aunt Bessie had taken the picture out of a dresser drawer where she had kept it folded in a white photograph album. Marty had handed the clipping back to her and she was replacing it in the album when another scene sprang into Marty's mind. A white album, much like this one, in a dresser drawer in the Perky's bedroom. Hansen, the caretaker, spying on her with toadlike eyes as she thumbed through it. The pictures of Lucinda in the nude and semi-nude. A snapshot taken in a nightclub. The girl had her head thrown back, laughing. Behind her shoulder, staring directly at her, was the face of a man. That face sprang out of her memory, almost with the impact of a blow. A solid, square-jawed face, topped by a shock of fair hair. Farr. She could remember the picture now in each detail, even to the lettering underneath. The Flame Club, May 21, 1959. So there it was in black and white. Her hunch had been right all along. Farr had known Lucinda.

Marty sprang to her feet. "Aunt Bessie, you're wonderful!" she cried.

The colored woman looked up in alarm. "What I done now?"

"No time to explain. I've got to run."

"Whe'ah you off to?"

"I've got to stop at the Perky camp to pick up something I'd forgotten all about until just this minute and then I'm going back to the prison. God bless you, Aunt Bessie."

3

She opened the door with the key Russ had given her. The lifeless house seemed even more creepy than the last time she had been there. Rank weeds had taken over the lawn and the small vegetable garden. The wind sighed through the pines like a lost soul.

Marty went back to the bedroom and pulled open the dresser drawer. Everything else was as she had left it, but the photograph album was gone. With a mounting sense of anger and panic, she began rummaging through the other drawers. Lucinda's nightgowns—all pink and yellow—were neatly arranged. Marty experienced a faint touch of queasiness as she handled the dead woman's things. Why no blue? she wondered idly. Don't snappy little blondes go in for baby blue to match their eyes? Well not this one apparently. There was no sign of blue anywhere.

Nor was there an album. After half an hour of frantic searching throughout the house, Marty was ready to face the bitter realization that the photograph, her prime piece of evidence, had been stolen.

4

The chief of police was named Ricketts. He was a rangy man, dry as worn whipcord, with the gaunt, graven face one finds so often among back-country Southerners. He had about him the air of an old dog or horse, patient and slightly put upon and faintly surly. Yet, at the same time, Marty was aware of his solid intelligence as she told her story.

"So you can see how important it is that I find it," she said.

The chief took a wrinkled package of Camels out of his pocket and said, "Yeah. I can see that all right. But what makes you so sure Hansen took it?"

"I can't be positive, but I know how interested he was in those pictures. He was the one who first told me about them. And so far as I know, no one has been in the place since."

"I don't like to accuse a man of somethin' he mebbe didn't do."

"Neither do I, but time is running out on me now.

That's why I came straight to you."

Ricketts nodded his Lincolnesque head gravely and said, "That was the right thing to do."

She was trying to control her impatience. She wanted to scream at him, *Well hurry, damn you!* but she knew now that none of these people could ever be rushed. He would have to take his own sweet time about it.

"Hansen ain't a member of the force," Ricketts said defensively.

"I know."

"Just works for us every now and then, like on these caretaker jobs."

"That's why I thought you wouldn't mind asking him about the album."

"Why hell no, I don't mind. Don't mind at all." He unwound his six-foot-three of narrow-hipped rawhide length from the chair and said, "He lives over to the hotel. We'll just stroll over there and have a talk with him right now." Marty knew the hotel. It was a square brick structure that was so monumentally ugly it hurt her eyes every time she drove past it. She had never been inside the building and she had always been vaguely curious about it, but now, in her impatience, she hardly noticed the grimy walls and the dark narrow staircase as she followed the chief up to the second floor.

He raised a big-knuckled hand and tapped it authoritatively on a door at the far end of the hall. Beside the door was a fire bucket half-filled with sand. Dead cigar butts studded this miniature desert like shattered palms on a shelled-out beachhead.

After a long moment they heard Hansen say, "Yeah?"

"It's Ricketts."

There was the squeak of mattress springs and then the slow shuffle of steps. The key turned in the lock and the door opened. Hansen stood there wearing only a pair of grimy, striped, underwear shorts. His hair was tousled and he was trying to rub the sleep out of his grainy eyes.

"Hell, Chief," he said plaintively, "what you want to wake me for? I was jus' havin' me the sweetes' dream. I was jus' …" His eyes widened a little when he saw Marty standing beside Ricketts.

"I want to talk to you, Hansen."

"Sure, Chief."

The skinny little man backed away from the door. His naked chest and shoulders were covered with an amazing forest of coarse gray hairs.

"What the hell's the matter with you, Hansen?" Ricketts asked in disgust. "Don't you see there's a lady here. Put yore goddamned pants on."

Hansen snatched a pair of pants from the back of the chair and thrust his skinny shanks into the legs. Marty followed the chief into the room.

Despite the heat the windows were closed. The air was fetid, sweltering. The bed was unmade and still damp with the imprint of Hansen's body. On the bureau stood a half-empty fifth of whiskey. Soiled clothing lay scattered and balled along the floor. The place was a rat's nest. But what was really surprising were the decorations. Hansen had what may have been one of the greatest collections of cheesecake art in history. Apparently, he had spent years clipping pictures of women in various stages of undress out of magazines and calendars. He had pasted hundreds of the pictures, rim to rim, over the walls and ceiling. Now there was no way to turn without beholding naked breasts, thighs, bellies and haunches. Like an astronomer studying the heavens, Hansen could lie flat on his back and gaze at an infinite variety of flesh.

The chief's distaste for the scene was evident. "You take somethin' from the Perky place?" he asked abruptly.

Hansen's little eyes darted back and forth from Marty to the chief. Obviously playing for time, he asked stupidly, "Who me?"

"They ain't but one Hansen here, is there? So it's you I'm talkin' to," the chief answered.

"What did you lose?"

"A book. A book of pictures, dammit."

"Not me," Hansen said. "I don't know nothin' about no book."

"If I had the time, I'd do this the easy way," the chief said. "But since the lady's in a hurry I got to speed things up." His big, thick-fingered hand darted out like a striking snake and gripped the brush on Hansen's chest. The chief twisted his hand and Hansen yelped in anguish, making a sound like a run-over dog.

"Hurry up," Ricketts said, "afore I pluck you like a goddamned chicken."

"Leggo. Leggo. You want the damned book so bad, I'll give it to you."

Ricketts released him and Hansen staggered back, rubbing his chest. "Didn't think a book of damned fool pictures was so all-fired important to anybody," he said plaintively. Still muttering to himself, he reached into a bureau drawer and pulled out the white album.

"That it?" Ricketts asked.

"I don't know. I'll have to check to make sure," Marty said.

She leafed through the book, feeling a small queasiness at having to touch anything Hansen had had his hands on, and quickly found what she was after.

"Mind if I take a look?" the chief asked.

She held the opened album across to him. He regarded the picture with cold blue eyes.

"It's that Perky woman, ain't it?"

"Yes."

"And that's Mack Farr with her. Now what do you expect to do with that?"

"I expect to prove that Mack Farr knew Lucinda Perky, and that he was in this area at the time of her death, and that he knew something about it."

"A little late for that now, ain't it?"

"If I can get a confession from Farr the governor will have to order a stay of execution."

"Farr is a pretty tough nut," the chief said doubtfully.

"Then I've got to find a way to crack him."

"Let's get out of this here hole," Ricketts said. "I need me some fresh air." He turned to Hansen and said, "Don't let me see you 'round no more. Next time I'm apt to take more'n hair off you."

When they had gone down the stairway and out onto the street, it was like emerging into a bright new world.

"I want to thank you for your help, Chief," Marty said.

"That's all right, Miz Waxman. I'm sorry about that Hansen."

"But you think I'm wrong in what I'm doing, don't you?"

"Yes'm."

"Why?"

"I still figure that fella Perky killed his wife."

CHAPTER TWELVE

The road to Miami, like any road in Florida that is more than a hundred yards from water, was hot and straight and deadly monotonous. Heading west from Belle Glade Marty kept the station wagon at an even 70. She knew that this was a killer stretch, that every year dozens of people died along there in flaming wrecks, but still it was out of season now and the traffic was light and the only real hazard was a blowout that might spin her into the canal, or one of the fuzzy-minded fishermen who now and then got so excited that they stepped straight back into the stream of traffic.

But as the miles went by, she became aware of another hazard. The accumulated tensions of the past few weeks were building up in her. Exhaustion nibbled rat-like at the edge of consciousness. The road swam before her in the hot haze and once she was brought heart-stoppingly upright by the chatter of her right front tire on the coral shoulder. She fought the car back onto the pavement and then pulled over into the next truck stop to gulp black coffee. At that point she decided it might be a good idea to put through a call to Miami to reconfirm her appointment.

"This is Mrs. Waxman. Is Doctor Kaufmann there?"

"The doctor is in consultation at the moment. Can I help you?"

"I just want to check on my appointment. I called early this morning."

"What time is your appointment for, Mrs. Waxman?"

"Two o'clock."

"Yes, that's correct. I have it listed right here."

"I'm calling to let you know I may be a few minutes late, I'm driving down from Okeechobee."

"Perhaps you'd like to change it. If you prefer I can give you the same time next week."

"Oh no. Please don't change it. This is a matter of the utmost importance. I must see the doctor today. Please make him understand that. I'm driving just as fast as I can, and with any luck I shouldn't be more than about fifteen minutes late."

"All right, Mrs. Waxman."

When she went back out to the car, the midday glare slashed at her like a whip. Even the dark glasses were not much help. She felt a bad headache coming on and thought of going back inside to buy some aspirin, but then decided that there was no time for it—she had better push on.

The plastic covering of the car seat was painfully hot. She let herself down into it gingerly and then wheeled the wagon around and waited for a big flame-colored tanker to go by before scooting out onto the highway. She was no longer sleepy, but the headache was growing more noticeable and she was conscious of an increasing pressure on the back of her neck, as if all the nerves in her body were being tangled into knots.

An hour later she had passed the turnoff to Hollywood and then she was in the outskirts of North Miami and fighting her way downtown through the traffic. She was only twenty minutes late when she pulled into the parking lot at the rear of Memorial Hospital.

Dr. Kaufmann's office was on the second floor. Apparently his nurse had gone out to lunch because the doctor answered the door himself. He was a small, undistinguished-looking young man who might have been taken more for a certified public accountant than a psychiatrist. Marty had never known a psychiatrist and somehow she had pictured him as an elderly, nearsighted type with thick-lensed glasses and beard.

"Dr. Kaufmann?"

"Yes."

"I'm Mrs. Waxman. I'm sorry to be late."

"That's all right, Mrs. Waxman. I know you've had a long drive. Won't you come in?"

They went through a small impersonal waiting room into the doctor's office. The black leather couch dominated the room. Since she was not there as a patient she took one of the small, hard backed chairs. The doctor sat behind his desk. He rested his elbows on the polished surface and put his finger tips together with the pensive air of a man who spends most of his waking hours listening to other people's troubles.

"As I told your girl over the phone, I wanted to talk to you about Maxwell Farr," Marty began.

The doctor nodded and said politely, "I found Farr to be an extremely fascinating case."

"When did you examine him, Doctor?"

"Actually there were two examinations. The first time immediately after his arrest and the second—oh, about ten days ago.

"Well as I told your nurse in our phone conversation, I think Farr may very well have some vital knowledge of another crime—one for which my client now stands convicted and waiting execution. I thought it just possible that Farr might have said something in his interviews with you that could be of value to us."

The doctor looked doubtful. "I don't recall his mentioning any other case, but of course I wasn't particularly thinking of it in that context. Naturally I'll be glad to help you in any way I can."

"Did he ever talk to you about a girl named Lucinda?"

"Not that I recall offhand. What was her last name?"

"Perky. Although he may have known her as Lucinda Clark, her name by a former marriage."

"Well, we can check it easily enough. I have the transcript of the interviews here." The doctor took a sheaf of papers out of a manila folder and leafed through them. When he looked up at her again, he shook his head saying, "I'm afraid not."

"How did you happen to interview Maxwell Farr, Doctor? Were you appointed by the court?"

"Not in this case, although I have done psychiatric work for a hospital criminal division. No, the interview was on my own time. I have been working on a book describing the characteristics of what might be called the rogue male, the man who is more or less at war with society. Farr seemed to be an almost perfect example of this type."

"In what way?"

Kaufmann hesitated and Marty pressed on. "Surely you can understand how important this is to me, Doctor. My client's life is at stake."

"I can understand that, Mrs. Waxman, but I don't really know what you hope to accomplish by questioning me about Farr."

"I'm hoping that you can give me some key to his personality, something that will produce an admission of involvement in the crime."

"I don't think it's that easy. There are no magic keys to personality. Often, even in the case of a skilled analyst, it takes years of interviewing to reach a given point in the subject's mind. And I'm afraid this would be especially true in a case like Farr's. As is so often the way with schizophrenics, he really has quite a brilliant and complex mind. Yet you seem to have the impression that you can reach the problem in one brief session."

Sensing that she was treading a bit heavily on the doctor's professional corns she tried to convey her desperation by saying, "But don't you see? I have no choice. This is absolutely my last resort."

"Then perhaps the best thing would be to read the transcript of the interviews," Kaufmann said in a soothing voice. "It might be best to do it in reverse, starting with the second one, since it is really more informative. In the first interview—which was done in the county jail only one day after he had been caught—he was very difficult. He was trying to demonstrate his toughness. He was reluctant to talk to me and his answers consisted largely of obscenities. In the second interview, however, taken at the state prison after his conviction, he was articulate and knowledgeable. He has a first-rate intelligence, and as you will see from the interview, he has made a thorough study of crime and punishment. Suppose I leave you alone with this material for ten or fifteen minutes and then, if you like, we can discuss it further."

As she leaned forward to take the folder, a wave of giddiness swept over her. The folder trembled noticeably and she had to steady herself against the desk.

"What is it, Mrs. Waxman? Are you ill?"

"Just tired, I guess. I've been on the go a lot and it was a long hot drive."

"When did you eat last?"

"Some time this morning."

"Some time this morning is not good enough," he said in tones of cold severity. "I'll have one of the nurses bring you a sandwich."

"I'm really not hungry."

"You have obviously been under a considerable strain and your system needs fuel. Now if you want my help, you must do as I say."

"You're treating me like a patient, Doctor."

"Well, that might not be a bad idea either, but we'll discuss that another time. Now, will you do as I say?"

"All right. I'll be good."

"Ham and cheese?"

She nodded.

"Fine. Now I'll leave you to get on with your reading."

She settled back in the black leather chair and opened the folder. The first page was titled: Second Interview With Maxwell Farr.

Q. Your full name, please?

A. Maxwell P. Farr.

Q. P for what?

A. P for pudding.

Q. P for what?

A. P for pudding. You look like a pudding puller from way back, Doc. All right, don't get your bollocks in an uproar. P for Peter. But tell me, why do we have to go through this jazz? You know my name. I guess you figure it establishes the proper level of cold-blooded analytical conversation. In that case let's do it right. Let me ask a couple of questions. What are your professional qualifications? Are you just some amateur head shrinker who's getting a charge out of talking to a real live criminal, or do you know what you're doing?

Q. I am a graduate of Tulane University. After receiving my degree in medicine, I was further trained in psychiatry at St. Elizabeth's Hospital, Washington, D.C. For three years I was a Fellow of the National Committee for Mental Hygiene. Following that I was Director of Mental Hygiene Clinics for the state of

Pennsylvania. For the past five years I have been Senior Psychiatrist at Memorial Hospital in Miami.

A. Okay, Doc. You pass. Carry on.

Q. What was your address before your arrest?

A. 24 Algonac Avenue, Trenton, New Jersey.

(Note: The above is typical of the subject's attitude. According to information later obtained, there is no such address. At the first interview he also gave a false address. Yet he is aware that his true address—112 East 14th St. New York City—is a matter of record.)

Q. Why do you persist in giving a false address?

A. Why do you persist in asking such bloody stupid questions?

Q. What was your father's occupation?

A. Doctor. Ordinary household variety of doctor. Not a faker like you. He was a nice enough old boy, but he never had much guts.

Q. How would you describe your mother?

A. Bitch.

Q. Your father is dead?

A. Suicide.

Q. Why did you kill the policeman?

A. Because the silly f— got in my way.

Q. But mightn't you have gotten away without killing him?

A. Possibly. Let's just say it gave me an enjoyable sense of power. Life and death s—. You, as a psychiatrist, must know that the need to kill is entirely apart from the motivations of ordinary crime. Or haven't you studied it?

Q. I have studied it.

(Note: Subject constantly attempted to reverse roles and assume attitude of interviewer. His knowledge of subject and air of authority made this easy for him. Interviewer was pleased to let subject express himself

freely in this manner.)

A. Then let me ask you a question, Doc. How do you feel about capital punishment?

Q. I am against it.

A. On what grounds.

Q. Moral grounds.

A. You mean you believe the state has no right to take a life for a life?

Q. Something like that.

A. Horse s——. The state has the same right as the individual.

Q. Aren't you afraid of death, Farr?

A. Now there's a stupid bloody question. All men are afraid to die. Do you know what Dostoevsky said about it?

Q. No.

A. He wrote that if in the last moment before being executed, a man, however brave, were given the alternative of spending the rest of his days on a bare rock with just enough space to sit down, he'd choose it without hesitation. And don't forget the old boy knew whereof he wrote because he'd spent a couple of bad minutes in front of a firing squad. So as one who also knows something about it firsthand and has made a pretty thorough study of it on the side—it makes a cute little hobby—let me tell you something about the psychology of murder. Did you ever hear of the Macdonell Report?

Q. I believe that was a study made in England some years ago.

A. That's right. Anyway, they came up with some interesting statistics. Ninety percent of the murders were committed by men and nearly two-thirds of the people they killed were wives, mistresses or sweethearts. The best day for murder is Saturday and the choice hours are between eight P.M. and two A.M. Thirty percent of the murders were brought about by drunkenness, quarrels and violent rage. Most of the rest were caused by jealousy, intrigue and sexual motives. Only ten percent of the murders were committed for financial reasons. Macdonell summed it up when he said that murder is not generally the crime of the so-called criminal classes. What he meant was that in damned few cases was it really premeditated. With most of them it was just the last and most violent in a series of violent acts.

Q. Are you telling me this to demonstrate something about your own behavior?

A. That's right. What I mean is that I didn't wake up that morning and say to myself, today I'm going to kill a cop. It just happened. The damned fool got in my way.

Q. Didn't you feel sorry for the man you killed?

A. Hell no. The man was a slob. What difference does it make if he lives or dies?

Q. It might make a difference to his family.

A. You mean some lousy c— waiting for a paycheck? To hell with her.

(Note: At this point subject's manner underwent abrupt transition. His air of breezy assurance was replaced by one of sullen depression. Along with his manner, his voice also underwent an abrupt change. From this point on his answers were delivered in a dull, monotonous tone. When discussing his relations with his mother he used the word c— repeatedly.)

Q. When did you first begin to hate your mother?

A. I don't remember.

Q. While you were still a child?

A. Yes.

Q. Did you resent her attitude toward your father?

A. Yes. She was always fighting with him and calling him names.

Q. Were there other things in her behavior that disturbed you? Was her behavior immoral in some way?

A. Yes.

Q. Did you ever see her with another man?

A. Yes. One summer we had a little house on a lake in Maine. My father could only get away from his practice on the weekends, and sometimes not even then. So during the week my mother and I stayed at the cabin alone. One day I went on an all-day hike with some other kids. But I developed a blister on my foot and came home early. There was a strange car parked at the end of the road. I went up very quietly to the house thinking I would surprise whoever was there. The living room was empty and the blinds were drawn in the bedroom. But one of the blinds had a little tear in it and by standing on tiptoe I could see through it. My mother was on the bed, naked. There was a man with her.

Q. Did you know the man?

A. I never saw him before. A big redheaded son of a bitch. The p— was slipping it to her right there in my father's bed.

Q. What did you do?

A. I walked back down the road to the village and I hitchhiked to New York. It took me two days to get there.

Q. Then what?

A. I went home.

Q. Did you tell your father what you had seen?

A. Yes. But he didn't do a thing about it. He was a sweet guy, but he had no guts.

Q. What did you think he should have done?

A. He should have killed the both of them.

Q. Did you and your father ever discuss it?

A. No.

Q. How old were you when your father killed himself?

A. I was eighteen. The first year I was away at college.

Q. The policeman you killed was tall and redheaded. Did you associate him with your mother's lover?

A. That's a lot of Freudian crap. But I don't know. Maybe in a funny way I did.

Q. In your first interview you referred to the policeman as "that big redheaded p—." These are almost the same words you used in describing your mother's lover. When did you first see that the policeman had red hair?

A. When I slugged him and he fell down and his cap came off. But if you think that's why I shot him you're nuttier than I am. If that was the case I'd have killed every redheaded guy I ever met. On the other hand, you may have something there, Doc. I never thought of it that way. As a matter of fact, I never even remembered that business with my mother until just now. But to hell with it. I don't want to talk about it anymore. To hell with it. To hell with you too, Doc.

(Note: The interview was terminated at this point when subject refused to answer any further questions.)

There was nothing else in the folder. Marty closed it and placed it back on the doctor's desk. At that moment the door opened and a girl in a pink uniform came in carrying a tray with a sandwich and a cup of coffee. Marty took the food from the girl and thanked her.

She was still toying with the sandwich when Kaufmann returned. "Finish your reading?" he asked.

"Yes. But I'd like to get more information on that

first interview. Can you tell me something about it?"

"Well it was pretty much more of the same. Except that he was rather more belligerent and less articulate. In a somewhat less obvious form it demonstrated the same division in his thinking—the conflict between the educated mind and the gangster's emotions. The mechanisms of symbology were equally clear."

Mechanisms of symbology. She hoped he would not embark on a roll call of psychiatric gibberish—she was much too weary to cope with it.

"You're not eating," he said.

"I'm trying, but it doesn't go down too well."

"I hope you're not planning to drive back today."

"I've got to."

"Well it's none of my affair, of course, but you really look done in."

"I'll be all right. The coffee will fix me up."

He shrugged. "As you like. If you want I can give you something to keep you awake."

She nodded. "That would be fine. But now let's talk about Farr. As I told you, I have reason to believe he may have been involved in another murder besides the one for which he is being held, and if I could prove that, it would save my client's life. Unfortunately, all I really have on Farr is a photograph showing he knew the murdered woman and the testimony of a witness who says that a man answering Farr's description was at the scene of the murder."

"I think I had better make my own position quite clear, Mrs. Waxman. This interview with Farr was not done at the request of the authorities; it was carried out strictly as part of my own research, and as such has no official standing. Nothing in it could be used as testimony. Wouldn't you be much better off to let the police handle this?"

"Certainly. But as far as the police are concerned the case is closed and they have no interest in reopening it. Anyway, there is no time for that anymore. I have only until tomorrow morning. That's why I'm pinning all my hopes on Farr. If I can break him down the governor will at least have to order a stay of execution. What I want you to do is to tell me the best way to tackle him."

The doctor shook his head. "I'm afraid it's more apt to be the other way around. As you can see from the way he dominated the interview, he is a very difficult man to maneuver. And utterly unpredictable. Everything will depend on the mood you catch him in."

"Is Farr insane, Doctor?"

"The court-appointed psychiatrist ruled him sane enough to stand trial."

"But what is your opinion?"

"His attitude toward society is manifestly psychopathic."

"Would a man in his condition be capable of a crime of this sort—a rape murder?"

"Obviously. He had the physical strength and the basic emotional ferocity. However, it doesn't quite fit in with his record. He has no particular history of sexual aberrations. I'm sorry I can't offer you more encouragement, or something more substantial, but there is really no magic word or mysterious key that will unlock Farr's personality. Let me sum it up like this—in many ways he is quite a superior person, a man of great intelligence and physical strength. Like all such people—born leaders—he is controlled by a superego. He sees himself in the Nietzschean context as a sort of superman. If there is a chink in his psychological armor, it is probably his vanity. By exploiting that you may get what you want from him. But again I must point out that it all depends on the mood in which you find him."

Marty knew that if she did not get up now she would fall asleep in the chair. She stood up and said, "I appreciate your help."

The doctor took a little bottle of green tablets out of his desk drawer and shook four of them onto his palm. "These are Dexamyl. If you take one each hour, they should manage to keep you awake."

"Thank you very much."

"May I offer you a word of advice?"

"Of course."

"Don't take this thing too hard. You look very tired, Mrs. Waxman, as though you may be pushing yourself too far."

The advice sounded empty. What did he mean, not take it too hard? What other way could you take it? "One way or another it will be over tomorrow," she said.

"Just don't expect too much of Farr. He is the type of man who can be diabolically clever if it happens to suit him at the moment."

"All right," she said. "Thank you again, Doctor."

On her way out she stopped at the drinking fountain and swallowed one of the Dexamyl pills. Backing out of the parking space she very nearly sideswiped a huge red-finned Cadillac. She was aware that her reactions were not what they should be. But by the time she was heading north on 27th Avenue, the pill was taking effect and she calmed down. She wheeled through the knot of traffic around Hialeah, then shot the car out onto the open road and pushed the speedometer up to seventy.

CHAPTER THIRTEEN

Russ fought against it, but the nightmare was on him. For the past two nights he had forced himself to remain awake to escape the horrible dream of dying, but at last exhaustion and the dream had overtaken him. He rolled from side to side on the bunk, and even in his sleep, a waxy sweat of fear appeared on his forehead. He cried out, but no one came to wake him. Tears squeezed between his closed lids rolled down his cheeks.

In his dream it was the morning of the execution and the chaplain was with him. The chaplain had a soft smooth voice and the prayers rolled from him almost like a song. Russ relaxed slightly, felt almost a sense of peace. But just then they decided to test the power. A switch was thrown somewhere behind the black door and the whole place was filled with a wild humming, like the sound of all the bees in the world. The lights went dim. Russ's heart tried to leap out of his chest.

A screen had been placed in front of the cell door so that he could not see what was happening, but still he could hear the tramp of feet and he knew that meant the witnesses were on their way to the place of execution. The noise made by these unseen men, the relentless scraping of their feet on the concrete, was somehow the most frightening thing of all. Russ swayed on his feet. He had very nearly fainted, hoped he would, but even oblivion was denied him. He was still sharply aware of everything when the screen was rolled back and the guards came for him.

He tried to clutch at the bunk, at the chaplain's

hands, at the cross those hands held, at anything that might give him an extra minute of life, but his nerveless fingers were pried away and he was half-dragged from the cell to the corridor where one of the guards cut two long slits in his trouser legs while another undid the top buttons of his shirt.

Then the hands that held him fell away and he summoned the last of his strength and was able to walk by himself toward the black door. But just before they reached it, as the door was swinging open on noiseless, well-oiled hinges, the thing he had been dreading happened. He lost control of his muscles and the stench of his filth soiled the air. He turned apologetically to the guards, but they walked straight ahead, seemingly unaware.

He paused in the doorway. Twelve feet away, it stood. Raw wood and naked wires and the limp black leather mask. So deep-rooted was his concentration on the chair that he hardly saw the faces of the spectators and the ventilator above the chair, cleverly designed to dissipate the fumes, and the bright light which would provide a clear view of his final agony.

"Have you any last request?"

The words seemed to reverberate throughout the silent room as if waiting for an answer, but he was unable to reply. Only by keeping every muscle clenched, was he able to maintain the strength in his legs. If he had opened his mouth to speak, he would have fallen to the ground.

Hands pushed him toward the chair and then down into the seat. Other hands quickly, expertly, adjusted the electrodes at his legs and wrists. In one abrupt, final motion the mask was lowered over his face. The black leather smelled of oil, of sweat, of tears. Only his lips and the tip of his nose were exposed. In his panic he bit down on his tongue. Blood spurted out of his mouth. His heart was racing like an engine gone wild. The warden raised his arm and then dropped it. Under the impact of two thousand volts Russ's head flew back as if he had been struck by a bullet and his body leaped against the straps. A curl of gray smoke rose from the top of his head and from his left wrist. The smoke was whisked away into the ventilator. His body still fought against the straps. His lips turned red, then blue. The air was filled with a sizzling noise and with the smell of burning flesh. He was being cooked alive.

After two minutes the current was turned off with a snapping sound, like that of a door being slammed. He sat motionless in the chair with his head hanging forward. Whatever flesh was exposed was bright red and swollen. Again the current was passed into the wires and once again his body fought the straps.

The big door slammed again and this time a doctor stepped forward and placed a stethoscope against his chest. There was still an indication of life. The heart still beat fitfully. Again the signal was given. Again the body leaped forward like a mechanical doll. His flesh sizzled and the smell of its cooking filled the air. The current was passed through him for another two full minutes.

"I pronounce this man dead," the doctor said in a grave voice.

The mask was removed. Russ's dead eyes glared crazily out of his swollen face. The tip of his tongue had been completely severed. Blood dribbled out of his mouth and down his chin. Two of the witnesses were noisily sick.

The straps were untied and the body was picked up and carried out.

Russ woke up screaming. One of the guards was shaking him. He sat up on his cot clutching at the slow realization that he was still alive.

Shaken, trembling, he tried to calm himself. He sat waiting for the pounding of his heart to let up. His shirt was black with sweat.

Suddenly he heard Farr begin to sing. The strong, unmusical voice filled the death house.

> Oh my name it is Sam Hall, Samuel Hall.
> Oh my name it is Sam Hall, Samuel Hall.
> Oh my name it is Sam Hall
> And I hate you one and all;
> You're a bunch of fuggers all—Damn your eyes!
>
> Oh they say I killed a man, so they said.
> Oh they say I killed a man, so they said.
> For I shot him in the head
> With a bloody lump of lead,
> And I left him there for dead—Damn his eyes!

The ancient ballad of the Tyburn Tree went on and on. Farr had made up his own version. His obscenities were enough to wake the dead. The guards bellowed at him to shut up, but he ignored them. If anything, their protests stimulated him. His voice rang out more strongly as he roared, "Damn your eyes; damn your eyes!"

Now the other prisoners were joining in. It was as if they had all been infected by a touch of madness. The bright lights were turned on, but the noise continued.

Very slowly, Russ felt his strength returning. The tremendous vigor of Farr's voice was irresistible. Timidly, at first, Russ began to sing. Then he heard Farr's bellow of encouragement. "That's the way, kid.

That's the way. Fug em all! Damn their eyes!"

"Damn their eyes," Russ sang.

CHAPTER FOURTEEN

1

Governor Harwood selected a shiny new Kro-Flite from the supply in his black leather golf bag and teed it up and sent a long straight drive down the fairway. He was conscious of approving nods from the caddy house. The governor's iron shots were nothing to rave about, but his woods were straight enough. He was grateful for that because it usually got him off the first tee in good shape, and that was where people were watching him.

The ball did not roll quite as far as he had expected. It was only a little past nine o'clock and the fairways were still heavy with dew. Harwood approached the ball and found it tucked into a little pocket in the wet grass. It was not a bad lie for a long iron—with that you could get into the turf behind the ball—but it was in too deep for a spoon. The governor resisted the temptation to improve his lie by edging the ball a couple of inches to the left, and asked the caddy for a number two iron, knowing even while he was still in the backswing, that he would club the shot. As a result of this foreknowledge, he raised his head at the last moment and topped the ball into the trap at the left side of the green.

The governor did not ordinarily go out to play golf on the morning of an execution. He would have considered this extraordinarily frivolous behavior on the part of some other government official. But he had spent a restless night wrestling with himself over the Perky case and had felt that he simply had to get some peace and quiet in the morning.

The governor had been forced to send four convicted men to their deaths during his term of office. Perky would be the fifth. He had not been happy about the other four, and now he was particularly unhappy about this fifth one. It was a terrible responsibility. Any moment now they would be calling him from the prison. If it were not for Robineau's downstate power....

He blasted the ball out of the trap and it soared to the edge of the green, rolling down toward the hole. It was quite a good shot leaving him only an easy downhill three-footer for his par four. All he had to do now was take it easy. That, he told himself sourly, was the way to get along. Take it easy.

As he climbed out of the trap onto the green, he thought again of the news he had heard yesterday. Judge Grady was dead. His body had been found in his car at the beach. What had Grady been doing alone in a car at the beach? It was not like him. It would have been more in character if he had been there with some woman. He had certainly never liked Grady, but now he felt rather sorry for him. It was an ugly way to die. And his death would certainly cloud the political picture. But, of course, there was still old man Robineau....

2

White boy go today, man. Ole warden try dat juice las' night. Hear dat hum? See dos lights dim? Ole warden tryin' out dat juice. Two thousand volts. Man, dey fry him like ole piece of bacon fat. Smoke come right out of dat chimney. Plenty of smoke when a man burn.

Hear dem sing las' night? Man, I hears it all de way over in dis ole Rock. Farr, he bellow like ole bull in fly time. My name, it is Sam Hall, damn yo' eyes. Hee. Ole warden hears it too. Hee.

How he gonna go, man? Do he go walkin', or does dey carry him? Do he crap his pants? Listen, man, when dat Farr go, he go walkin' all by hisself. He spit right in dat warden's eye. But dat white boy, Russ, him dey got to carry.

You wants to bet on it, man? Hell, you got nothin' to bet with. Got dis ole sack of terbaccer. How you bets, den? Bets you dey got to carry him. Dat what you say? Stick of thaw to sack of terbaccer say he go like a man.

3

There was desperation in Marty's voice as she asked, "Do you understand, Ben?"

The guard shook his head. "It's absolutely against regulations, Mrs. Waxman."

"Do you think at a time like this I can worry about regulations? Look, Ben, I'm not giving you any choice. Do you understand?"

"I understand," he said solemnly.

"All right then. Now here is what I want. Just ten minutes alone with Farr where no one can hear us. I don't care how many guards are watching us, but I want to talk to him out of their hearing."

"But I tell you there's no way I can work that."

"Isn't there an exercise area in back of the death house?"

"Sure, but that's out. We're not going to put you any place where Farr can get his hands on you. Anyway, the warden will be coming through that way, and if he sees you there with Farr, God knows what will happen. No, if you talk to Farr, it's got to be with wire between you."

"That's all right. I don't care about the wire."

"Then I'll try to arrange for you to talk to him in the interview cage."

As they approached the main gate, the metals detector buzzed like an angry snake. The gate guard put out his hand to Marty and said, "What are you carrying, lady?"

"I don't know. Nothing."

He shook his head. "The machine don't lie. You got something there lady. Let's see your bag."

She handed over the bag and the guard opened it and took out a small flat plastic box, not much larger than a transistor, "Now what do you call that?" the guard asked.

"That's a tape recorder."

"Better open it up."

"But there's no time. There's a man's life at stake here."

"I can't help that," the guard said stubbornly. "You can't pass unless I know what's in there."

"Do you know how to open it, Mrs. Waxman?" Parker asked.

"I just bought it yesterday. They told me how to operate it but that was all."

"Let me see it. I've been fooling around with radios ever since I was a kid." Parker took the tiny German-made machine out of the guard's hand and after a moment's manipulation, opened the back so that they were able to see down into the maze of wires, transistors and tiny batteries.

"Now ain't that somethin'?" the gate guard said. "A

sure enough tape recorder no bigger than your hand."

"Please," Marty said. "We're in a terrible hurry."

"Okay, lady. Okay."

The gate opened with agonizing slowness.

With Parker at her side, Marty moved quickly along the walk past the mess hall and the tobacco factory toward the death house. The place seemed curiously still. The yard was deserted and this time there was no music. Because of the execution that would take place this morning, the men had been locked into their cells and a brooding air of expectancy had settled over the prison.

When they had reached the door Parker said, "You go in there to the interview cage. I'll bring Farr out to you."

Marty settled down in front of the wire screen, her heart racing.

"Is there an open phone to the governor's office?" she asked the guard at the desk.

"Should be."

"I want to check it."

He indicated the instrument with a wave of his hand and said, "Help yourself."

But at that moment she saw Parker and Farr coming toward her from the other side of the screen. She fumbled hurriedly into her purse to click on the tape recorder and turn the volume up full. With her other hand she clipped the tiny microphone, no bigger than a button, to the outside of the bag. Without taking her eyes off Farr, she said over her shoulder to the guard, "Won't you be a good fellow and call the governor's office for me? Tell them you're calling for Russ Perky's attorney. Ask them to have the governor standing by."

"Okay," the man said reluctantly.

A moment later Farr's cold blue eyes were gazing

out at her through the screen. She was wondering how to begin with him when the guard who had been using the telephone called out to her, "The governor ain't there. They say he's out playin' golf."

4

Now Russ's dream was reality. The chaplain, grave-faced, his shoulders bowed, as if under the heavy weight of death, came quietly into the cell. His voice was no more than a whisper. The guards in the corridor averted their eyes. Finally a screen was placed in front of the cell door.

Russ's teeth were chattering. "Mack," he called out. There was no answer from Farr.

"Mack! Where are you?"

Still no answer. He felt utterly alone. Not even Parker, whom he had considered his friend, had come to be with him at the end. Tears streamed out of his eyes and ran down his gaunt cheeks. He began to throw himself back and forth against the bars like a mad animal. The chaplain said helplessly, "My son. My son." Then three of the guards rushed into the cell to hold him. They did not want him to injure himself. A man going to his death at a public execution is supposed to be in good shape.

5

"Well hello, sweetheart," Farr said. "It's nice to see you; but aren't you in the wrong pew? You're supposed to be with your boy in his final half-hour."

"I wanted to talk to you."

"I'm flattered. You'll have to forgive the surroundings," he said with a wave of his hand. "No soft lights and sweet music."

"You knew Lucinda Perky, didn't you?"

Farr's laughter rang against the iron walls. "So that's it. Your last time at bat. And you struck out, kid." His laughter stopped as suddenly as it had begun and he said in his mocking voice, "Sorry to disappoint you, honey, but you're barking up the wrong tree."

"Am I? What about this?" She pulled the photo of Farr and Lucinda out of her briefcase and held it up for him to see. The whir of the tiny tape recorder in her bag seemed to be growing louder. She hoped Farr would not hear it.

"So she kept it. Why, the sentimental little bitch," Farr said.

"Do you still say you didn't know her?"

"Oh, I knew her all right. But what of it? So did a lot of other guys."

"Where did you meet her?"

"Like the picture says—the Flame Club in Detroit."

"Were you in love with her?"

"I don't know about love, but I do know she was the best-looking piece I ever saw in my whole damned life."

"And you killed her."

"Now why would I want to do that?"

"You raped and killed her."

"For your information, Duchess, nobody had to rape Lucinda. Nobody except maybe her own husband."

"But you admit that you knew her that well."

"Sure. What of it?"

"And when you found out where she was living, you came down here after her."

"Did I?"

"You were jealous of Russ. You hated him all along. That's why you were glad to see him die for a crime he didn't commit."

"If you say so, sweetie."

"Tell the truth, Farr. For once in your life and before it's too late, tell the truth!"

He looked back over his shoulder in the direction of the corridor and said, "It's too late now. They've already taken him out."

She fought back the rising tide of panic and said grimly, "Then you might just as well tell me all about it."

"Why sure," he said in a surprisingly eager voice. "As long as it can't do that bastard Perky any good, I don't mind getting it off my chest. It was this way. When I first knew her, she was married to some other poor sucker. They had split up and she was working at the Flame Club. I had just come back from Korea and I had a wad of back pay saved up and I used to go in there every night...."

6

The governor was one over par on the first hole and bogey two on the second. He stood on the third tee looking at the cup-shaped green 185 yards away. This was his favorite hole, well-suited to the player who could hit a short, straight, well-lofted ball with a spoon or number four wood. Harwood felt reasonably confident of his par three on this one or perhaps even a birdie two. Someday, he thought with satisfaction as he addressed the ball and looked down the lovely stretch of fairway to the flag whipping in the wind, I will hole out here with a perfect drive.

His wrists felt strong and his body was loose and easy. He had that comparatively rare inner conviction that he was about to make a fine shot. Perhaps today is the day, he thought, when the ball will just catch that little hill on the far edge and roll sweetly and inevitably down to the pin. So strong was this feeling that he almost called to the caddy to go forward to take out the flag.

He waggled the club head tentatively and took one more look toward the green. But just as he was about to start his backswing, he realized that he was not concentrating on the ball. Instead, his eyes had strayed to his wrist watch. The golden watch embedded in the short crisp hairs of his wrist read nine thirty-five. Only twenty-five minutes to go until the warden gave the signal that would convulse Perky forever.

The full knowledge of his own lack of responsibility smote the governor. How could he be out here playing a game while another man died? A political opportunist he might be, but had he really sunk this low? To hell then with old man Robineau and Dicky Miller and the dead Grady.

The governor never completed his backswing. Instead, with a decisive gesture, he bent down and picked up the ball and signaled the caddy to follow him. The startled boy looked back to see the governor, who was ordinarily so dignified, running wildly toward the clubhouse.

7

As he was being dragged down the corridor, Russ's last shred of pride and self-control deserted him. Screaming with fear, his bowels open, he was clutching at anything he could get his hands on. The guards struggled to pry his fingers away from the bars while the other prisoners stared silently out at the grotesque, tortured man.

Word had already been flashed to the Rock that those who had wagered he would turn chicken at the end had won their bets.

8

"... Then I was away for a couple of months and when I came back to Detroit she was gone. Nobody seemed to know what had become of her, although there was some talk that she had remarried. I tried to forget her, but it wasn't easy. I had to find out where she was. If she had married again, it had to be in the records. I went down to City Hall and found it. She had married some jerk with the silly name of Perky. So I checked a little further and found that they had moved to a fishing camp in Florida.

"Quite a while went by before I decided to do anything about it. Then one day I woke up and knew I had to see her. I hopped a plane to Jacksonville and picked up an old heap and drove out to the place. When I got there she was alone. She said her husband was out fishing. She was wearing a kind of blue dressing gown with nothing underneath. She had put on a little weight and she looked better than ever.

"I had to have her, and I asked her how about it, but she said no. She said those days were over. She wasn't giving it away anymore. She had found out that there were men who would pay plenty for it, and that was the way it was now.

"Well that threw me. She hadn't been any virgin when I first met her, but she was no whore either. I got sore as hell, and after I had finished yelling at her, I jumped into one of their damned boats and went out onto the lake to cool off. But I hadn't gone very far before I knew what I would do.

"I turned the boat around and when I was a hundred yards away from the place, I shut off the motor and rowed back to the dock. Then I sneaked up to the house and got in through the back door to the kitchen and waited for her. When she came in from the bedroom, I grabbed her. She tried to fight me off, but I was too strong for her. I ripped that blue dressing gown off and got her down on the floor. I was holding her around the throat to keep her from screaming. She was fighting me all the way, but when I got her legs apart she quit fighting.

"When it was over, I knew she was dead. I didn't feel anything about it. She was a bitch and a whore and she had gotten what she deserved. I knew nobody had seen me come in or out, and there was nothing to identify me with the place, so I just left her there on the floor and ducked out.

"I felt so safe about the whole thing, I didn't even make a run for it. Instead, I just hung around town waiting to see what would happen. Next morning it hit the front pages. They had found her and they had arrested that silly little bastard Perky. That was the funniest part of all. I had hated her, and I had hated that damned little slob who had taken her away from me, and now I had finished them both off together.

"But in a way it kind of backfired on me. I guess I got a little overconfident after the Lucinda thing, and I was short of dough, and I tried to knock over that garage, and killed the cop. Well what of it? Anyway, none of it matters now. Your boy is dead."

She did not wait for his last sentence. She was already reaching for the phone and shouting at them to put her through to the governor.

Time was like a knife at her heart. Each fraction of a second drove the steel deeper.

"This is Governor Harwood," said the deep, quiet voice.

9

"Parker! Stop them! The governor—I've got the stay!"
Her voice cracked. She could not have uttered another word. But Parker was already running for the black door. She ran after him, bursting out of the corridor into the death chamber, only half-seeing the row of faces and the warden's startled glance, but then focusing with shocking intensity on the cone of light and the man slumped forward in the chair with the mask over his face.

It was too much. Shadows rolled toward her. She sank to the floor. As from a great distance, she could barely hear Parker's voice saying, "It's all right. It's just that he fainted. They haven't pulled the switch."

With a sigh, she let herself go. The fog covered her.

CHAPTER FIFTEEN

"What about my tennis racket? Will I need that, Mommy?" Meg asked holding up the bright red child-size racket.

"I think so, dear," Marty answered.

"But the strings are broken."

"We can have it fixed."

"Are you sure people play tennis in Aruba?"

"I'm sure they do."

"What kind of people are they?"

"Mostly Dutch."

"Are Dutch people nice?"

"Of course."

"I still don't know why we're going there."

"I've tried to explain it to you, Meg darling; but if it didn't take, I'll do it again. Aruba is a pretty little island off the coast of South America. They have very little water there, and for that reason things don't grow well, and they have to import all their food. The government of Aruba has heard about Daddy's work here in hydroponic farming, and they have invited him to come down there to try the same thing. If it's as successful as we expect it to be then Daddy will build farms in other places as well. It's what Daddy has been working so hard for."

"Will we have a nice house?"

"A nice big white house right on the beach. It's the house I showed you in the photograph."

"Do you speak Dutch, Mommy?"

"No, darling."

"How will we talk to them?"

"We'll learn some of the language. And, of course, most of the people there speak some English."

"I'm glad we're going away from here."

"So am I, darling. But it was something we had to do, and now it's behind us. Is there anything else you want to go into the trunk?"

"I don't think so."

"What about your books?"

"Just my favorites. Just *Heidi* and *The Wind in the Willows*."

"All right, slowpoke, go and get them."

While Meg rummaged in the toy cupboard, Marty began going through the desk, discarding old letters and receipted bills. Dan came whistling merrily into the room, saw the pretty target she presented as she bent over the desk, and gave her a hearty slap on the rump.

"Hey! That hurt. What do you think I am? An English barmaid?"

"I don't know. How is it with English barmaids?"

"You're feeling pretty cocky, aren't you?"

"Darn right I am."

"All right, little man, you've certainly earned your big moment. I guess you have a right to enjoy it."

"They said it couldn't be done...." He started to hum, and then broke off to ask, "When do they come for the trunk?"

"This afternoon. I'm sending it collect. Will that be all right?"

"Sure. De Jong will take care of everything. VIP treatment, you know."

"Oh, shut up." She listened for a moment and then said, "Isn't that a car turning in?"

"Sounds like it."

"Who is it?"

"Surprise, surprise. Russ Perky."

Her face was apparently the mirror for her thoughts because Dan, who was watching her, said, "What's the matter? Don't you want to see him?"

"I don't know."

Since his release, more than a month before, she had not heard from Perky, and for her own part she had made no effort to get in touch with him. This reluctance to see him had puzzled her, but she had not been able to arrive at any clear explanation for it. Was it out of a sense of delicacy, or was it simply the aftereffect of the shocking experience they had both undergone? Perhaps there was something more, something that nudged at the back of her mind and made her uneasy.

"You take him out to the porch, Dan," she said, "while I put Meg to bed."

"Do I still have to take a nap today, Mommy?" the little girl asked. "Even though we're leaving tomorrow?"

"You sure do, honey."

She undressed Meg and took the pale blue ribbon out of her hair and pulled the little blue nightgown over her head. Suddenly, a light clicked on in a dark closet of her memory. She was back again at the Perky camp the day she had gone there to look for the missing photograph album—the hot, closed-up room, the wind in the pines, her frantic search through the dresser drawers, Lucinda's filmy nightgowns neatly folded just as she had left them—froth of pink and yellow, not a blue one anywhere—and she could remember now her slight feeling of surprise. Didn't blondes go in strongly for baby blue? Well what of it? Why was it important? In some way that she did not yet understand, it had to do with her reluctance to see Russ again.

As she drew the blinds in the bedroom and turned on the air conditioner, Marty was remembering her last conversation with the chief of police. It had taken place while they were going through the formalities attached to Russ's release from prison. The big-fisted, hard-eyed policeman had said, "It don't make no nevamind to me, Miz Waxman, but I still think they made one helluva mistake."

"How do you mean?" she had asked.

"Farr never done it."

"But we had his confession."

"The man had to die anyway. What difference did it make to him? They could only burn him once."

"Are you trying to say the confession was a lie? That he did it just to save Perky?"

"Somethin' like that."

"But he thought Perky was already dead when he confessed."

"I'll admit he cut it pretty fine, but mebbe he done it that way just to make it sound convincin'. It was one helluva gamble he took, but he sure pulled it off. Now the way I see it is Farr knew her all right. That much of his story was true. And he come there to see her just like he said. But there was one big difference. When he got there she was already dead."

"You're wrong, Chief. Farr hated Perky."

"Hated him enough to save his skin. Could be I'm wrong, Miz Waxman, but the way I see it, that Perky got hisself a free ride."

Stubborn man. She thrust it out of her mind and went out onto the screened porch where the two men were sitting over cold beers. Russ had changed. He had put on weight and the boyish look was gone. His jowls were heavy and there was a definite thickness around his middle. As he thrust out his hand to her, he had an air of breezy assurance that she found vaguely disturbing. He looked, she thought, like a prosperous salesman of second-hand automobiles.

"I heard you were leaving and I wanted to say goodbye," he said.

"That was nice of you, Russ."

"I would have been over sooner, but things have been so darned busy around the camp, I just couldn't get away."

"I'm glad your business is good."

"Good, hell. It's terrific. It's funny, ain't it, how business has picked up since I got out? It's like they all heard about the place because of the trial and everything, and they come there out of curiosity or something. Why one guy yesterday even asked me to show him the exact spot on the floor where they found her body, so he could take pictures to show his wife and kids."

"Did you show him?" Dan asked.

Russ shrugged. "Why not? Business is business. Anyway, that's what I wanted to talk to you about, Mrs. Waxman. You never did send me a bill." He pulled a thick wallet out of his back pocket and said, "How much do I owe you?"

"You don't owe me anything. There is no bill."

"How come?"

"I'm not particularly proud of the way I handled your case, Russ. I don't want to charge you for it."

"Oh, come on now."

"No, I'm not a lawyer anymore. I've given it up. I've decided that one career in a family is enough. From now on, I'm just a housewife."

"Okay then," Perky said quickly, "but your husband here is a witness that I tried to pay you."

He still held the wallet loosely in one hand. They could see its bulging contents. A corner of one of the bills was showing. It was a hundred-dollar bill.

"Business must be *really* good," Dan said.

Russ looked down at the wallet and said with a smile, "Oh the money ain't all from the camp. It turned out Lucinda had quite a wad of her own. She had it tucked away and I just kind of stumbled on it. I guess that sort of makes me her natural heir, don't it?"

When no one said anything, Russ asked, "Did you hear about the way Farr went?"

"No," Dan said.

"I was up there to see it."

"You saw Farr's execution?"

"Sure. At first they didn't want to let me in, but I told them it was the least they could do for me after everything they put me through."

Dan coughed heavily and blew out a cloud of foam. "Sorry," he wheezed. "Beer went down the wrong way."

"You got to admit old Mack the Knife had plenty of guts," Perky went on. He walked into that there room and sat down without a quiver. Then he looked right over at me and he busted out laughing like it was all the biggest joke in the world. When the warden asked him if he had any last thing to say, he just said, 'Why sure, Warden. Damn your eyes.' Now ain't that something?"

"Yes," Marty said in a small voice. "It certainly is."

"Russ, did your wife ever have a blue dressing gown?"

"Why?"

"Farr said she was wearing a blue dressing gown when he killed her."

He gave her his best boyish smile. "Farr must of been color blind. Lucinda never had no blue dressing gown as long as I knew her. She hated blue. Yellow was her color. Well it's nice to see you folks, but I got a lot to do. I guess I better be running along now. Have a good trip."

They heard his car shift into second and then into high. The sound of its exhaust faded. They had not exchanged a word. The silence was deafening.

THE END

BASIL HEATTER BIBLIOGRAPHY
(1918-2009)

Fiction
The Dim View (1946)
The Captain's Lady (1950)
Sailor's Luck (1953)
Act of Violence (1954)
A Night Out (1956; expanded from "The Empty Fort," 1954)
The Trouble With Love (1960)
Any Man's Girl (1961)
The Mutilators (1962)
Virgin Cay (1963)
The Better Part of Valor (1964)
The Naked Island (1968)
Harry and the Bikini Bandits (1971)
The Scarred Man (1973)
Devlin's Triangle (1976)*
The Golden Stag (1976)*
Bitch (1979)
The Einstein Plot (1982)
The London Gun (1984)

*Tim Devlin series character

Young Adult Fiction
Wreck Ashore! (1969)

Non-Fiction
The Black Coast: The Story of the PT Boat (1967)
The Sea Dreamers (1968)
Eighty Days to Hong Kong: The Story of the Clipper Ship (1969)
Against Odds (1970)
A King in Haiti: The Story of Henri Christophe (1972)

Short Stories
The Dim View (*Liberty*, Dec 14 1946; published as novel)
The Last Raid (*Cosmopolitan*, Nov 1946)
Island Happy (*The Saturday Evening Post*, Sep 23 1950)
Strike at Madang (*Argosy*, Nov 1950; *Trap of Gold and Other Great Adventure Stories from Argosy* 1952)
Hunter's Moon (*The Saturday Evening Post*, Nov 4 1950)
The Empty Fort (*Manhunt*, Sept 1954, expanded as *A Night Out*)
The Ghost of Old 21 (*Adventure*, March 1957)
The Big One (*Argosy*, Oct 1957)
Ladies of the Night (*Argosy*, Feb 1958)
Night Fight (*Redbook*, April 1958)
The Lady's Choice (*The Saturday Evening Post*, Jan 1959)
The Pirate of Prospect Park (*Argosy,* Jan 1959)

Basil Heatter, the son of radio commentator Gabriel Heatter, was born on Long Island on March 26, 1918. He attended schools in Connecticut, then went abroad when was 16 for a two year travel stint through Europe. Returning to America, he went to work for a New York advertising agency. He enlisted in the Navy in 1940 and during WWII served as a skipper on a P.T. boat in the Southwest Pacific. Besides being a news commentator himself, Heatter wrote twenty novels of intrigue and adventure—beginning with *The Dim View* in 1946, the story of a young PT boat skipper—as well as several non-fiction works revolving around his love of the sea. In fact, he lived for years off Key West on his own self-built sailboat, *The Blue Duck*. He died on June 12, 2009, in Miami, Florida.

Made in United States
North Haven, CT
06 February 2026